Dunston Falls

Dunston Falls

Al Lamanda

FIVE STAR
A part of Gale, Cengage Learning

Detroit • New York • San Francisco • New Haven, Conn • Waterville, Maine • London

Set in 11 pt. Plantin.

Printed on permanent paper.

LIBRARY OF CONGRESS CATALOGING-IN-PUBLICATION DATA

Lamanda, Al.
Dunston Falls / Al Lamanda. — 1st ed.
p. cm.
ISBN-13: 978-1-59414-586-5 (hardcover : alk. paper)
ISBN-10: 1-59414-586-5 (hardcover : alk. paper)
1. Sheriffs—Maine—Fiction. 2. Women—Crimes against—Fiction. 3. City and town life—Fiction. 4. Maine—History—20th century—Fiction. I. Title.
PS3612.A5433D86 2007
813'.6—dc22 2007041330

First Edition. First Printing: March 2008.

Published in 2008 in conjunction with Tekno Books and Ed Gorman.

Printed in the United States of America
1 2 3 4 5 6 7 12 11 10 09 08

For Brenda, Kim and Nicole.
Thanks for all your support.

PROLOGUE

Somewhere between midnight and one a.m., the ice began to fall. It was a fine mist at first, followed by pea-size pellets. It quickly covered the ground and trees in a layer of frozen ice. By one-thirty a.m., the pellets swelled to golf-ball size and anybody who was awake knew they were witnessing something special. A once in a lifetime, winter weather phenomenon, people on the news would later observe and report. Earlier that night, on the weather forecast, those same people called for precipitation, maybe some freezing rain. They couldn't have been more wrong.

What followed was the storm of the century. From as far south as the Jersey shore, it stretched in an isolated band to Montreal, Canada. It was nature at its most beautiful and most deadly form.

It would be the topic of conversation for weeks. On television, on talk radio and in the newspapers, people could not get enough of the ice storm. They were stunned that the contemporary world in which they lived shut down so quickly and with such ease by a source they could not control. Nature, they seemed to have forgotten, controls the planet in spite of the ego of those who dwell upon it.

Most who experienced it learned a valuable lesson in life. Others never seemed to learn anything.

Most people were fortunate and survived just fine. Others did not. Some were not aware the storm even occurred at all.

One

When Sheriff David Peck opened his eyes, he was not conscious of what woke him from a deep and sound sleep. He lay still for a minute, listening to his own breathing, fine-tuning his senses. He rolled over in his bed to check the time on the alarm clock on the nightstand. It was just a bit past two-thirty in the morning. As he lay there in darkness, he slowly became mindful of the sound, which woke him. His eyes moved to the window on the left side of his dresser. There was a soft, plinking noise as if someone on the outside were tossing rice against the glass. It took a moment before he realized the noise was caused by ice crashing against the bedroom window.

Tossing off the covers, Peck stood up and crossed the bedroom to the window to look out. A layer of ice frosted the glass, making it impossible to see anything on the other side. Turning away from the window, he clicked on a light and grabbed his robe, then went downstairs to the first floor.

In the living room, Peck picked up his cigarettes from the art-deco–style coffee table, lit one and walked to the front door where he switched on the outside floodlight. He was unprepared and totally surprised by the sight which greeted him when he opened the front door.

Hail the size of golf balls crashed to the ground at a furious pace. In the driveway of his small home, Peck's 1955 police cruiser was already under an inch-thick layer of growing ice. The six inches of snow on the ground glistened from its new, frozen blanket as it reflected light from the floodlight. Small trees such as white birch bent halfway to the ground under the stress of their added, unrelenting, ice-covered burden.

Remarkably, there was little if any wind and the ice fell in a straight line to the ground, which caused it to pile up even more quickly. He did a quick check on his memory, searching for storm bulletins. The best he could remember was a snow warning from the south that the storm was heading north.

Chilled and getting wet, Peck closed the door and entered the kitchen where he turned on a large radio, which rested on the counter near the sink. Being as far north as he was, there was little reception except for emergency weather broadcasts out of Augusta. He twisted the massive dial until a local station, filled with static, finally came in. An update from the monitoring station in the town of Gray gave details of the pending winter storm. An advisory was in effect until morning. A thirty-six-hour window before the storm actually passed was in effect, but road and travel conditions would make any chance of a normal commute next to impossible. Advice was to stay indoors until the governor lifted the advisory and road crews had the chance to clean up the roads.

Peck turned off the radio, poured a glass of milk from the refrigerator and smoked another cigarette at his green and yellow kitchen table. Like most committed bachelors, Peck knew how to cook, but spared himself the unpleasant task. He survived mostly on cold cuts and by eating out. Such a lifestyle kept his needs to a minimum and the kitchen was barren of most domesticated appliances.

He sat for a while, smoked and thought about the storm. If it followed the predicted path, conditions would be harsh and the situation would present his first real challenge as sheriff.

By three-fifteen, he was back under the covers. He wasn't tired, having gotten that second wind which comes from getting out of bed. He listened to his breathing and could feel his heartbeat begin to slow. Then his eyes grew heavy, as he was lulled to sleep by the continuous, rhythmic sound of ice plinking against the window.

Peck awoke for the second time that morning at just before seven a.m. He rolled out of bed and glanced at the radio alarm clock on the nightstand. The time had stopped at four ten a.m. He clicked on the lamp and nothing happened. Power lines were down from the storm, probably. Not a good way to start the day.

Wearing his robe, Peck went downstairs to the living room where he loaded the woodstove centered in the room with logs and old newspapers and lit a fire. His coffeepot was electric so he filled a pan with ice from the refrigerator and boiled it on the woodstove to make instant coffee. Filling a second pot with ice cubes, Peck used the water to wash his face and brush his teeth.

As he sipped the instant brew, Peck tried to call his office from the kitchen wall phone, but the phone lines were down as well as the power. Entering the living room, he sat before the warmth of the woodstove, smoked a cigarette and thought for a moment. On his desk in the corner of the room was a large, battery-powered civil air defense radio, which was on the same frequency as the radio in his office.

Peck went to the desk, sat down and cranked the handle of the radio. "This is Sheriff David Peck. Is anyone there? Over," he said into the base-held microphone.

There were a few moments of static before Jay Bender, Peck's lone deputy answered.

"Dave, this is Jay. Over."

"Jay, what did you do, walk? Over."

"A tenth of a mile, it took me almost an hour. Over."

"What does it look like out there? Over."

"Like Alaska in the wintertime, what did you think? Over."

Peck lit a cigarette, took a sip of coffee and thought for a moment. "How does it look for driving? Over."

"Driving? Only a fool or a native of Maine would attempt it. Wait, isn't that the same thing. I was you I would stay put. Over."

"I'd like to make it in and keep an eye on things. I can always sleep in the office. Over."

"Good luck. I'll keep a fire burning and the coffee hot. Over."

"Just don't burn the office down before I get there. Over."

"I was a boy scout, remember? Over."

"Maybe you could scout us up some breakfast. Out."

Wearing a yellow slicker over his winter uniform jacket, Peck carried a pot of boiling water to his black and white patrol car where he used it to melt enough ice to open the driver's side door. He returned to the house for another pot of hot water to melt the thick layer of ice on the windshield and rear window. He started the engine, and then let it run for fifteen minutes. He used the time to boil more water to fill a thermos with instant coffee. Returning to the cruiser, he inspected the heavy chains around the snow tires before entering and putting the car into gear.

Even with the chains, the heavy car skidded along the ice-covered road as he turned out of the driveway. Within minutes, a coverlet of ice blocked the rear window, making rear visibility impossible. The front windshield fared only slightly better. Peck had to run the defroster and wiper blades on high to maintain any visibility at all. Then, cautiously, he crept along.

One hour and five minutes later, Peck drove the cruiser across the lone paved road, which led to the center of town. A sign the size of a stop sign and mounted on the curb off Main Street read WELCOME TO DUNSTON FALLS, MAINE, est. 1889. Pop. 311. Stretched across Main Street, a large banner read, Happy New Year 1959. The banner was rigid and covered in a sheet of ice.

As Peck approached the municipal building, he passed the town's only drugstore, library, church, diner, gas station and hospital. As he expected, nothing was open for business. The place was a ghost town.

Parking nearly on the curb, Peck exited the cruiser and dashed into the municipal building. The building was the only two-story, red-brick structure that was not a private home within the boundaries of the forty-seven-square-mile town. The first floor contained his office, a small holding cell and a tiny office for the part-time tax assessor. The second floor housed the office of the town manager, Ed Kranston. Void of working light bulbs, the hallway was dark and cast in shadows.

Removing his ice-soaked yellow slicker, Peck entered his office. There were two green metal desks, his and the one belonging to his deputy, Jay Bender, who was stoking the fire in the woodstove when Peck walked in. Otherwise, furnishings were sparse, just the bare necessities to run the office.

"I see you made it," Bender said as he shoved a log into the woodstove.

Peck removed his jacket and tossed it on the chair behind his desk. "Is there any news out of Augusta?"

Bender stood up, closed the door to the woodstove and stretched his back. He was a young man of thirty, tall and lanky, with a baby face that appeared never to need shaving. "The report out of Gray says the storm might go a week. I can't reach Augusta."

"A week of this and we'll all be living in igloos."

"It's not just us. All of New England, parts of Canada."

Peck sat behind his desk, feeling the wet from ice residue

behind his shirt collar. "We need to get in touch with Ed and . . ."

"He's here, in his office."

Peck was surprised. "He walked?"

Bender reached for the stainless-steel camp-style coffeepot, which was boiling on top of the woodstove and poured himself a cup. "Just because we are in the sticks doesn't mean we have to live in the sticks, Dave."

Peck picked up the mug on his desk and held it out for Bender to fill.

"Sorry, Dave, no donuts," Bender said.

Peck lit a cigarette with a match, blew smoke and looked at Bender. "The phone lines are down. I thought they were on separate power lines."

Bender grinned as he carried a mug of coffee to his desk. "Amazing how a few million tons of ice fucks up the works, isn't it."

"What does the governor's office have to say?"

"Officially, that they're doing all they can. Unofficially, pretty much that we're fucked until otherwise notified."

Peck and Bender turned their heads as the office door opened and Ed Kranston stepped in. He paused to look around. "Well, this is cozy. A nice fire, hot coffee."

Bender grinned. "Want some?"

"You have donuts?"

Ed Kranston was a large man of sixty, who never wore anything but a well-tailored suit. He had thinning, brown hair and wore rimless glasses. His blue eyes were piercing when angry and aimed in your direction. His smile was equally as powerful and could charm the scales off a snake. As was his custom, he was chewing a stick of gum.

"Got a Hershey bar," Bender said, opening his desk drawer. "And a stale pack of cookies."

Peck set the cigarette in an ashtray as he sipped from his mug. "Is there anything new out of Augusta, Ed?"

Kranston lowered his bulk onto the chair opposite Peck's desk. It creaked under his weight. "I reached the state police on the shortwave in my office. Power is out as far south as Rhode Island, as far north as Canada. They figure at least a week, maybe ten days. Phone lines, too."

Peck picked up his cigarette and took a puff. He blew a smoke ring as he mulled over the situation in his mind. "What do we got, three hundred plus living in town?"

"Three eleven, according to last year's tax assessment," Kranston said. "Probably a couple more now. Hard to say."

"Every home has at least a woodstove for heat and possibly cooking, but people won't be able to last ten days without fresh food and hygiene," Peck said.

"Or medicine," Bender added.

"Especially medicine," Peck said as he crushed the cigarette in a tin ashtray on his desk.

"What are you suggesting?" Kranston asked.

"An emergency alert is out unless power is restored," Peck said. "Right?"

"No chance of that," Kranston said. "Not for at least a week. And even if we could broadcast on the emergency alert system, how many radios would pick it up?"

"What do they have for rooms in the hospital?" Peck said.

"Twenty-six," Kranston said. His eyes brightened. "But the basement can hold another fifty, not to mention the waiting room and lobby. That's at least a hundred people, maybe more."

"What about the church?" Bender said. "There's plenty of room in the basement and halls."

Kranston turned around in his chair to look at Bender. "That's at least another hundred. That's very good thinking, Jay."

Bender nodded and said, "But without the shortwave or television, how do we reach anybody? Forty-seven square miles is a lot of . . ."

"Door to door," Peck said. "We go door to door."

"In what?" Bender said. "The cruiser? It took you an hour just to drive here in that piece of junk. We'll never make . . ."

"We have two snowmobiles sitting in the basement garage not doing much of anything," Peck said. "We can use them."

"That's right," Bender said. "And extra gas cans we keep for the cruiser. We can use them."

Peck looked at Kranston. "Talk to Doctor McCoy and Father Regan. Tell them we want to use the church and hospital as emergency shelters. We will need blankets, cots, water and food. Also, ask Deb at the diner if she can run a generator for hot food."

Kranston nodded. "Tell people to bring whatever they can carry of their own food. The diner will run out pretty damn quick otherwise."

Bender stood up from his desk and walked to the door. "Meet me in the basement in ten minutes, Dave. I should have them running by then."

Kranston also stood up. "I'll try the shortwave again before I talk to McCoy and the priest."

"Remind me to hit you up for two new snowmobiles in next year's budget," Peck said.

"I thought you wanted a second deputy?"

"I'll settle for one of each."

After Kranston exited the office, Peck opened his bottom desk drawer and removed two large walkie-talkie radios. Power came from four large batteries, which he inserted into each unit.

Satisfied the radios were working properly, Peck spun his chair around and looked at the large map of Dunston Falls, which hung on the wall behind his desk. The borders of the forty-seven-square-mile town were marked in red. Most of the land, undeveloped, was property of the Great Northern Paper Company. Sprinkled throughout the interior were several hundred homes where paper company employees lived. The lone paved road that ran north to south cut directly through the heart of the small town square and looped around in a circle.

Peck took a sip of coffee as he studied the map. After eighteen months of living in Dunston Falls, he knew he was still a novice when it came to knowing the cut of the land. Even a native could easily lose his way in a storm, much less a city boy like him.

Before he left the office, Peck used the tiny bathroom in the hallway. He stood in the dim light and inspected his face in the mirror. The fifty-three-year-old man who looked back at him appeared surprisingly unaffected at having spent twenty-seven years as a Baltimore cop. The bags under his eyes were hardly noticeable, as were the creases in his forehead. His chest was firm, his stomach was flat, and the muscles in his arms bulged with the strength of his youth.

Turning away from the mirror, Peck slipped the yellow slicker over his jacket and left the bathroom.

In the basement garage of the municipal building, Peck and Bender stood before the two late-forties-model snowmobiles. They were massive machines and their engines roared loudly in idle gear. Dark smoke filled the enclosed garage, making it hard to see and breathe.

Peck waved a hand at the smoke. "Jesus."

Bender said. "We picked them up from the warden service a few years back when they got approved to buy new ones. They run better in cold air."

"I'm amazed they run at all. What are they, ten years old?"

Peck handed Bender a walkie-talkie. "Call every thirty minutes, if possible."

Bender nodded. "I know the layout better than you, Dave. I'll take the south and west where the homes are deeper in the woods. If you stay on the north fire roads, you should hit maybe thirty homes. Most of them are trailers without woodstoves."

Peck agreed. "With a little luck, I'll meet you back at Deb's for dinner."

Bender mounted a snowmobile, put it in gear, gunned it and raced up the exit ramp to the street.

Peck waited a moment, the older bull in not so much a hurry as the younger one, then climbed aboard his snowmobile. He put the machine in gear, and then gently guided it up the exit ramp to the street.

Peck accepted the hospitality of the Johnson family and stepped inside to warm himself by the fireplace and sip the hot chocolate Mrs. Johnson prepared by boiling milk in a pan over the fire.

Mr. Johnson's first name was William and he went by Bill. He and his wife had two small children, who he supported by driving a truck for the paper company. Their home was a three-bedroom Tudor that was set back a hundred yards off a fire road. Bender was right, if you didn't know the layout of the land, homes like the Johnsons' could be easily missed.

Peck said, "It would be better if you could get the kids to the church or hospital for a few days. Bring food, blankets and whatever water you can manage."

Mrs. Johnson shook her head. "We don't have a portable radio, Sheriff. How much longer is the storm expected to last?"

"The weather service said another week, but power could be down for several weeks to a month," Peck said in between sips of hot chocolate.

"Weeks to a month?" Bill said. "We don't have enough food

to last that long."

"Nobody does, but the hospital has a freezer and so does the diner," Peck said. "We'll manage."

"I'll start packing," Mrs. Johnson said.

Bill turned to his wife. "Don't forget that case of Coca Cola in the basement. At seven cents a bottle, we might as well drink it."

Peck handed Bill his cup. "Thanks for the cocoa. I'll see you in town."

Peck drove the snowmobile down a long, ice-covered dirt road on his way to his tenth stop of the morning. By the time he reached the driveway of Deb Robertson's home, his slicker was encased in a frozen layer of ice. He shook it off, feeling like a wet dog as he walked up the two flights of steps to the front door.

Deb Robertson opened the door before Peck knocked. "I heard the snowmobile," she said. She was a slim and very attractive woman of forty-five, with shoulder-length dark hair and gray eyes that were positively haunting.

Peck pulled the hood of the slicker off his face and stomped his feet to get some feeling going.

"What are you doing out in weather like this, Sheriff?" Deb said.

"This storm. We have a statewide emergency. People need to be notified."

Deb held the door open for Peck and stepped out of the way. "For God's sake, come inside before you freeze to death."

Logs crackled in the stone fireplace as Deb poured Peck a cup of coffee in the living room, where he sat on the sofa. Although rustic in design, the home contained every modern appliance and convenience of the day. Somehow, Deb managed to bring together the old and the new and make it fit so her home had an engaging and comfortable feel to it, like an old-style bed and breakfast.

"I have a generator," Deb explained. "I've been running it every two hours for fifteen minutes." She poured a cup for herself and sat down next to Peck on the sofa.

"I have enough firewood out back to last until spring, so I'm not worried about myself."

Peck sipped the hot coffee, felt it warm his stomach. "Can you run the diner by generator?"

"For as long as the gas holds out, maybe a week."

"We'll need it," Peck said. "We're setting up the hospital and church as shelters. We could have as much as two hundred people living in town by tonight. What do you have for food in storage?"

"I just had a delivery. Several weeks of frozen, a month of canned goods, but there is no way I can make it there in this."

"I'll stop back before dark and give you a lift."

"Wait. Don't go just yet. It's so . . . creepy without the radio or TV. Just that ice hitting the roof. Not even a wind." She nodded her head toward the massive television against the wall, which was more a piece of furniture than anything else was in the room. A large screen, color probably, was encased in a walnut cabinet with doors that were presently closed and polished to a high shine.

Peck followed her eyes to the television cabinet, which looked like an RCA, then he looked at Deb and she smiled at him. "I still need to reach a lot of people before dark," he said.

Deb reached for the coffeepot, which rested on a coaster on the coffee table. "Five minutes won't make a bit of difference." She refilled Peck's cup and her own.

"Okay to smoke?"

"Sure."

Peck removed his cigarettes from an inside pocket and lit one.

"I quit," Deb said. "Ten years ago, but I could pick one up like it was five minutes ago."

"So did I, but I started back up again."

"How come?"

Peck thought for a moment. "I don't know," he admitted. "Old habits die hard, I guess."

Deb nodded her head. "What time will you pick me up?"

Peck glanced at his watch. "Four okay?"

Deb nodded. "Don't be late."

The sun was low in the dark sky when Peck reached Fire Road 99. The barrage of hail made it difficult enough to see in daylight. After dark, it would be impossible. He turned the snowmobile around and headed back to Deb Robertson's home.

During the fifty-minute drive to her home, Peck's mind began to wander a bit. Deb Robertson was a very attractive woman and the way she smiled at him led him to believe she might be interested in more than just a ride to town. He toyed with the idea and reached the conclusion that his imagination had taken a turn down the wrong way of a one-way street. This was a time of emergency and stress levels were on high; it was only natural she might appear overly responsive and more friendly than normal. As he neared her home, Peck dismissed the idea from his mind and concentrated on the task before him, ensuring the public's safety.

When Peck arrived at her home, Deb was dressed and ready to go. She wore a full-length winter raincoat, snowmobile boots and a plastic scarf covering a winter hat. "It isn't glamorous, but it's dry," she said of the scarf.

Deb hopped on back of the snowmobile and held Peck around the waist. "Hold on," Peck said as he gunned the engine.

Driving along the slick, ice-covered dirt roads, Peck was aware of Deb's hands around his waist. Even through his heavy jacket, they had a warming effect. He was uncertain if she knew what he was feeling, but he decided to keep it to himself.

Forty-five minutes later, Peck slowed the snowmobile to a stop in front of Deb's Diner. She climbed off and smiled at Peck. "My bones are rattling. Can you do me a favor and go around back and start the generator?"

Peck spun around to the rear of the diner where a large generator sat inside a wood hut against the building. He parked the snowmobile, used a log to smash through the ice, and opened the door of the hut. He primed the engine, put the generator on start and pulled the cord. It started on the third pull, smoked and sputtered a bit, then roared to life.

Satisfied the generator would run, Peck mounted the snowmobile and drove to Main Street where he parked in front of the hospital. Dim light from candles was noticeable from the street. Peck shook off ice and entered the hospital through the front entrance. Dozens of town residents were milling about, looking to settle in. Some knew him by name and greeted Peck as he walked through the lobby to the small hospital lounge. Entering the lounge, Peck found Doctor Tom McCoy at the table. Two candles burned for reading light as McCoy scribbled notes on a pad. He took a sip of coffee from a mug and looked at Peck.

"It isn't good, but it's hot," McCoy said.

Peck lifted the metal pot from the burner behind McCoy and filled a mug, then took a seat at the table opposite the doctor.

"How many have showed up so far?" Peck said.

"Maybe thirty, but they're still rolling in."

"What can you squeeze out of your generator?"

McCoy glanced at his pad. "I was just figuring that. At two-hour intervals, I have enough gas for three days."

"And no woodstove for backup."

McCoy shook his head. "This is a hospital, not a hunting lodge." At thirty-five, McCoy was slim of build and average in height. His sandy hair was medium in length, his brown eyes soft in nature. His ears were a bit too large for his face, but not unappealing to look at. "It's going to get cold in here when the gas runs dry."

Peck removed his cigarettes and lit one. He mulled the situation around in his mind. "We have some gas cans in the basement garage, but it's not enough to run the hospital and church for more than a day or so extra."

McCoy stood up to refill his mug. "I could use it."

Peck said, "I've been out all day. Is there any news on the storm?"

The lounge door opened and Father Regan walked in. "I just had my transistor radio on. It's going to get worse before it gets better," he said. "And by the way, does anybody have some extra nine-volt batteries?"

"I might have some," Peck said. "I'll check. If not, it might be a good idea to get the drugstore open."

"I have an extra key around here someplace," McCoy said. "I'll take a look and give it to you, Dave."

Peck nodded.

McCoy filled another mug with coffee and offered it to the priest. Regan took a sip and made a face. "That's awful, Tom."

"But hot," McCoy said.

Regan took a chair next to Peck. The priest was a tall man of fifty, with broad shoulders and no fat on his waist. His thinning hair was brown and speckled with gray. A twinkle shown in his blue eyes that had a calming effect on his parishioners, as did his soothing voice.

"How are you doing, Father?" Peck said.

"I've got three dozen families living in the church basement.

I need cots, blankets, food and heat, but most of all heat."

"How are you on gas?"

Regan shook his head at Peck. "Not nearly enough. Three days if I conserve."

"Conserve," Peck said.

McCoy sat down and looked at Peck. "We have to be able to do something other than conserve, Dave. Maybe we can send somebody to the paper company for help?"

"That's a forty-five mile trip," Regan said. "Each way. No one will make that in this storm."

"Yeah, but they have those trucks which could drive through anything. They could load up on supplies and be here in two days," McCoy said.

"I could try to reach them by radio," Peck said. "In the meantime, we have to do whatever we can to make sure people are safe. That means we do whatever it takes."

Father Regan and McCoy looked at Peck. In unison, they nodded their heads.

A fire crackled in the woodstove in the corner of Peck's office as he lit a cigarette and looked at Bender and Ed Kranston. Warmth radiated from the stove and spread throughout the room, raising the temperature to a comfortable level.

Bender sat behind his desk and doodled on a pad with a pencil. Kranston occupied the chair opposite Peck's desk. Peck looked across his desk at the town manager and waited for him to begin the conversation.

"My bones," Kranston complained. "Something happens to a man when he turns sixty. It seems impossible to get warm." He removed a fresh stick of gum from his pack and placed it in his mouth.

Peck reached into the bottom desk drawer for an unopened bottle of scotch. "Will this help?"

Kranston looked at the scotch. "That's the bottle I gave you for Christmas."

Peck removed the seal and twisted off the cap. "Got any glasses, Jay?"

Bender opened a desk drawer and removed a sleeve of plastic cups. "From the Christmas party," he explained.

Peck poured two fingers of scotch into three cups, and then gave one cup to each man.

Kranston tossed his gum into a trash can, then took a shallow sip of the liquor and grimaced. "Next year, remind me to get you the good stuff."

"I wouldn't know what the good stuff is on a cop's pension." Peck lit a cigarette and turned to Bender. "How many candles we have left?"

"A box of a dozen," Bender said. "I can probably get more from the church if we need to."

"I seem to remember a kerosene lantern around here somewhere," Kranston said.

"I think it's in the tax office. Want me to check?" Bender said.

Peck nodded and Bender stood up and left the room.

Kranston took another sip of scotch. "The batteries in my shortwave went dead. I can't contact Augusta or anybody else for an update."

"Mine are low, but I got enough for a few more calls. I can always bring it to the hospital and run it off the generator."

"Good idea. Speaking of the hospital, what's the situation look like?" Kranston asked.

"By tomorrow, a hundred people in the hospital and church. It's going to get crowded, but at least it will be warm and the food will be hot for a while."

"Hot?"

"Deb's running the diner off a generator for as long as she can."

Bender returned with a kerosene lantern. "Got it." He struck a match and ignited the lantern, then blew out the burning candles.

Kranston shook his head. "Hygiene is going to be a mess. With just a few bathrooms and no running water, it's going to get ugly quick."

Bender sat behind his desk, opened a drawer and removed a Hershey bar. "Remember the state fair we had for the Fourth?"

Kranston turned to look at Bender.

"Those six portable toilets we rented," Bender said. "Remember?"

"We can't exactly rent them in . . ."

"No," Bender said. "We never returned them. They're still sitting in the garage over at the landfill. Nobody ever came to pick them up after they were emptied and cleaned."

Peck leaned forward in his seat. "That's right."

"I'll see which good ole boys got their trucks next door and go pick a few up," Bender said. "We could set two in back of the church and hospital. Maybe another out back of Deb's."

"Excellent," Kranston said.

"Might as well get started," Bender said.

"Bring your walkie-talkie," Peck said. "I don't need you getting lost out there in this."

Bender picked up his walkie-talkie, stuck it in his jacket pocket, grinned at Peck and left the room.

"He's turning out to be a fine deputy," Kranston said. "I had my doubts at first, but not anymore."

Peck nodded his agreement. "I hesitated to hire a man without experience, but Jay has proven to be a fast learner with a good feel for the job. We might want to consider a raise for him."

"When this is over, maybe we'll talk about that. First, and as soon as we're able, I want to call a town meeting to talk about a revision to the budget," Kranston said. "We need to be more proactive in our emergency planning, even if it means higher taxes."

"Higher taxes?" Peck said. "Come on, Ed, gas is up to thirty cents a gallon as it is. Cigarettes are what, forty cents a pack?"

"I know it, but there is no other way to generate the income we . . ."

Peck held up his right hand. "Hold on, Ed. I just thought of something. We don't need the generator at the church to run during the day, do we?"

"I suppose not. Why?"

"I can have it moved to the gas station to run the pumps and fill the gas cans. We can power the hospital, church and diner for weeks."

"He just got a delivery the other day, didn't he? Those tanks should be close to full. Good idea, Dave."

"I have another good idea, Ed. Let's find out what Deb has on the grill. You can finish telling me about higher taxes over Deb's meatloaf."

It was a full house at the diner. All twenty tables and the dozen counter stools sat occupied. The dishwasher, a Mexican named Paco Ramirez, acted as a messenger to the church and hospital, informing town residents of empty tables. Father Regan and Doctor McCoy assigned seating arrangements to keep things orderly. Everybody, it seemed, did their part to make things as comfortable as possible while they rode out the storm.

Peck and Kranston shared a table near the window. There was nothing fancy about the diner. It could have been one of thousands anywhere in the country. Tabletops were green, the counter held a dozen backless stools. The order of the day was

Deb's prized meatloaf special with gravy and mashed potatoes. Peck resisted the temptation to ask her for seconds, opting to fill his stomach with bread and a slice of apple pie for dessert.

As Kranston sipped coffee, he studied Peck. "I knew it was the right move bringing you in, Dave. Remember our first meeting?"

Peck looked up from his apple pie. "Yes, I do."

Eighteen months ago, Peck met Kranston in Cole Farms restaurant in the small town of Gray, some six hours south of Dunston Falls. Peck made the trip from Baltimore the previous day, stayed over in a small motel in the nearby town of Windham and then met Kranston for their planned luncheon meeting. For a small restaurant in the middle of nowhere, the pot roast was excellent and Peck had seconds.

Kranston had a copy of Peck's resume and cover letter. "I'll be honest with you, Mr. Peck. I was surprised and pleased when thirty-five police captains and detectives like yourself answered my ad for sheriff. However, not a one of them was as honest and forthright as you were in your letter."

"I appreciate that, Mr. Kranston," Peck said.

"No, I do. It makes my choice rather easy." Kranston picked up Peck's resume and studied it briefly. "You spent fourteen years as a patrolman, thirteen years as a detective in vice and homicide. You retired as a lieutenant. Dozens of citations and awards, it is all very impressive. However, what struck me is what you said in your letter. That you were applying for the position simply because after two years in retirement you were bored."

"That's true and I am," Peck said.

A waitress stopped by to refill their coffee cups.

"Where else can you get coffee for a nickel with unlimited refills?" Kranston said.

"Your ad said this is a new position, Mr. Kranston. Is that correct?"

"Yes. Dunston Falls is a very small town, Mr. Peck," Kranston said. "However, it sits on a vast amount of land owned by the Great Northern Paper Company. Do you know anything about paper?"

"It's good for writing," Peck said.

Kranston smiled. "True, but in today's modern era, it is used more and more for things like paper plates and party goods, frozen dinners and so on. That means expansion. That means Dunston Falls will grow and we need to grow along with it."

"You want a police force in place before you need it, rather than need it and not have it," Peck said.

"Exactly," Kranston agreed. "But, it's more than that. The wave of the future is upon us and it is in one hell of a hurry. Ten years ago, I did not own a television set. Today, I have a color one, even though ninety percent of the programs are in black and white. I need to modernize my town or it will be left behind, I'm afraid. Like you said, it's better to have than need."

"I can appreciate that," Peck agreed. "Before I left the department, all kinds of new procedures and equipment were being tested. It used to take weeks for an FBI lab to match a set of fingerprints. Now, they can do it in a matter of days. By the mid-sixties, who knows what they'll be capable of?"

Kranston took a sip of his coffee and looked at Peck over the rim of the cup. "I notice that ring you wear isn't police."

"No, it's Army," Peck said.

"You served during the war?"

"Three years in the Pacific."

Kranston set his cup aside and folded his hands on the table. "Let me be honest, Mr. Peck. The position only has a budget of one hundred twenty-five a week, but you get to live rent free in a completely furnished, very comfortable home."

"The salary is fine, Mr. Kranston. I have a decent pension after twenty-seven years," Peck said. "And I'm glad the house is furnished because I don't own much."

"Good. Now, what do you know about Maine?"

"I can find it on a map."

Peck's recollection ended when Deb approached the table with a fresh pot of coffee.

"No more for me," Kranston said. "I'll have trouble sleeping as it is."

Deb looked at Peck and he nodded his head. She filled the cup, and then slid onto a chair next to Peck. "I have to get off these feet."

Kranston stood up. "I'm going home and get some sleep. I suggest you do the same, Dave."

"Last cup," Peck said. He suddenly became aware of Deb's knee against his leg. Feeling like some stupid high school kid, he left his leg against her knee and it felt comfortable.

"You wouldn't happen to have a helmet of some sort?" Kranston said.

Peck shook his head. "Put it on next year's budget."

"I can get you a spaghetti pot from the kitchen," Deb said.

"I'm not walking down Main Street with a pot on my head."

Peck grinned at Deb. "She's right, Ed. That hail has a sting to it."

Deb stood up. "I'll make it a nice one without too many dents."

Peck stifled a laugh when a minute later, Kranston left the diner with Deb's spaghetti pot on his head. From behind the counter, Deb grinned, and then rejoined Peck at his table. "How long do you think it will take Ed to go deaf from the hail bouncing off that pot?" Peck said.

"My guess is about thirty seconds."

Grinning, Peck said, "Are you going to run the place all night?"

"All night, or until everyone is fed, whichever comes first. Either way, I'm here for the duration."

"I'm going to the office," Peck said as he stood up. "If you need a ride home, come get me."

"Paco has his truck, but maybe you could pick me up tomorrow?"

Peck nodded and walked to the door. "Save me another slice of apple pie for later. I may need it."

After making a roaring fire in the office woodstove, Peck assembled a cot from storage near his desk. He had a lumpy pillow and a green army-type blanket. After stripping down to his underwear, Peck sat at his desk to smoke a cigarette, eat a second slice of apple pie and wash it down from a plastic cup with one finger of scotch in it.

He took his time, sipping the scotch, tasting its blend on his tongue. When his eyelids began to droop, Peck tucked himself in, and fell asleep listening to the logs in the fire crackle.

Some time later, Peck opened his eyes when something woke him up. He did not know what that something was. In the background, the fire still crackled in the woodstove, so he could not have been asleep for very long, maybe an hour.

Peck shifted his weight in the uncomfortable cot, closed his eyes and was about to drift back to sleep when from the street came the loud crack of a rifle shot. He bolted up and out of the cot in a heartbeat and ran to the desk for his pants and shirt. As he was strapping on his sidearm, another rifle shot sounded. Stepping into his boots, half out of his jacket, Peck ran out of the office to the steps of the municipal building. Removing the flashlight from his belt, he scanned the immediate area. The beam of light from the flashlight glistened in the falling ice.

Across the street in the hospital window the light of a candle suddenly appeared. With hail falling all around him and sticking to his hair, Peck walked down the steps and crossed the street. He was halfway to the hospital as another booming rifle shot sounded, echoing loudly. Peck ran to the curb as another loud crash boomed in the distance.

A dozen town residents exited the hospital and stood under the protective awning, which extended nearly to the curb. Doctor McCoy was out front of the group and spotted Peck.

"What the hell was that, Dave?" McCoy shouted.

"I don't know," Peck admitted.

"Sounded life a rifle," somebody in the group said.

"A rifle shot?" McCoy said. "Who in the hell would be firing a rifle in the middle of the night in this weather?"

As dozens of town residents now occupied the street, Father Regan joined Peck and McCoy. "What's happening?" the priest wanted to know.

At that moment, another loud crack sounded, followed by a thunderous boom.

Peck stepped forward. "It's coming from the woods."

"He's right," somebody said. "I think it's the woods to our left."

McCoy looked at Peck. "Somebody's in the woods with a gun? In a storm like this, I find that hard to believe."

An old man stepped forward and stood next to Peck. "Listen."

Peck looked at the old man. "Listen to what?"

The old man moved out to the street, away from the shelter of the awning. His eyes lifted upward, above the line of sight of the town and toward the woods. After a few moments, he turned and stared at Peck. "It's the trees," the old man said.

Another loud crack sounded, followed by an echoing crash.

"It's the trees," the old man said. "They're falling."

A hundred yards past the line of Main Street, a pine tree, covered in thousands of pounds of ice, brittle from its frozen burden, snapped in two and fell to the ground a hundred feet below. As it broke apart, its fragments produced the crisp sound of rifle fire. When several tons of frozen wood hit the earth below, it shook the ground with a thunderous, echoing boom.

Peck turned his head to look at the old man. "He's right. It is the trees."

McCoy stepped forward. "I think this would be a good time to get back inside."

Peck turned to the crowd. "Everybody, back inside where it's safe. There's no sense in freezing or getting hurt."

The crowd dwindled until Peck was alone with Father Regan. "You, too, Father. Inside, please."

Regan smiled at Peck. "The power of nature is nothing more than the power of God."

"No disrespect, Father, but the power of God is going to drop something pretty damn heavy on your head if you don't get inside."

Regan nodded. "Goodnight, Sheriff."

For the second time that night, Peck sat at his desk with a finger of scotch in his plastic cup and smoked a cigarette. The woodstove crackled lightly in the background. The only light source in the room came from a single, thin candle on his desk. Suddenly, from outside came another loud crack, followed by a thunderous crash. Peck winced at the noise as if in pain.

Minutes passed without another tree falling. Peck lit another cigarette and as he smoked, his eyes went to the tiny flame of the candle. He followed the flame as it flickered and danced as hot air from the woodstove moved across the office.

A haunted, lifeless expression washed over Peck's face as he stared at the flame. His eyes did not blink until the cigarette in his lips burned to the filter, then he snatched the singed butt and squashed it in an ashtray.

He took a final sip from the plastic cup, and then added another ounce from the bottle. In the distance, another tree cracked loudly and hit the ground with a thunderous crash.

He smoked another cigarette as he finished the scotch. The cot near the woodstove beckoned to him and he finally gave in to his exhaustion and returned to it for some much-needed sleep.

Before his eyes closed and his mind set for some much-needed rest, another tree cracked loudly outside. When it hit the earth, Peck felt its vibrations in the cot. Then silence settled in and he fell asleep.

Two

Peck woke at first light with a stiff back and aching knees from a bad night's sleep in a cot too small to accommodate his large body. He tossed the army blanket around his shoulders and went to the window to look out. The ice was falling faster and heavier than the previous day. Main Street was a skating rink, a glistening sheet of smooth ice.

After loading the woodstove with logs and igniting a fire, Peck prepared the stainless steel coffeepot with water from the gravity-fed cooler and set it on the flat surface of the stove to percolate. By the time he had dressed, the coffee was ready and Peck took a mug to his desk.

As Peck lit a cigarette, Kranston entered the office.

"Good morning, Dave. Did you hear that last night?"

"Only all night."

"Must have been a hundred trees came down," Kranston said as he poured himself a mug of coffee. "It will be a miracle if no one is hurt."

In the background, there was the loud crack of another tree giving way to the ice and Kranston looked at Peck. "Make it a hundred and one. Well, at least the paper company will benefit from all this."

"Maybe, but it isn't safe anymore, Ed," Peck said. "We have to reach as many people as possible today and get them into town."

"I agree. If you and Bender could carry my shortwave across

the street to the hospital, I will run it off the generator and contact Augusta. Maybe we can get some supplies from the National Guard."

Peck glanced at his watch. "He should be here by now."

The door opened and Bender walked in, carrying a paper bag. "I am here, Dave, and I brought breakfast. Compliments of Deb's Diner."

"She's here already?" Peck said.

"Not already," Bender said. "She never went home. She slept on a cot in the diner."

"What have you got there?" Kranston said, looking at the paper bag.

"Egg and bacon sandwiches, corn muffins with jelly and some whatnot." Bender set the bag on Peck's desk and removed the contents. He looked at Kranston. "And she wants to know who's picking up the tab for all the food the town is eating."

"I'll ask Augusta for emergency funds," Kranston said, reaching for an egg sandwich.

"Which is what every town in the state will do," Peck said.

"And they will get it from Washington," Kranston said. "By the time the red tape is cut, it will be spring, but the money will be there."

Peck looked at Bender. "Let me have one of the whatnot, then let's hit the road."

One hour after eating breakfast, Peck found himself at the junction of Fire Road 99. He turned onto the road and drove the snowmobile at a medium speed. According to the tax records, at least two homes were located on the long stretch of dirt road. The first home, a mobile trailer, belonged to a widow named Doris White. She was forty-seven years old and worked in the payroll department of the paper company. She lived alone. Peck had never met her, or if he had, he didn't recall the meeting.

Suddenly, a tree snapped in half directly over Peck's head and he gunned the snowmobile as it fell to the ground with a loud crash. It was a tall, thick, white birch, about a thousand pounds of frozen wood. It missed Peck by ten feet. He brought the snowmobile to a stop, dismounted, and stared at the fallen birch tree. The son of a bitch would have killed him instantly had it found its mark.

Turning around, Peck spotted the trailer home of Doris White thirty yards to his left. A giant pine tree, brittle with ice, had come down and crushed the tiny home under its enormous weight. Peck left the snowmobile and ran to the home. The massive tree was directly over the center of the aluminum roof, separating the home into two parts.

An old Ford pickup, maybe a '47, covered in an inch-thick layer of ice sat just out of range of the tree. From the thickness of the ice on the windshield, he estimated the truck hadn't been started in days. Peck went around the truck to the side of the mobile home and peered through an ice-covered, dark window, but he couldn't see inside. He removed the revolver from his holster and smashed the window with the butt. Carefully, Peck climbed through the broken glass and entered the trailer.

Inside the dark, small living room, Peck used his flashlight to guide him through the debris and rubble to the bedroom. The brunt of the tree had hit the roof directly over the bedroom, making it impossible to pass around it and enter.

Peck crouched down on the floor and shined the flashlight under a slab of collapsed wall toward the bed. At first, he wasn't sure. Then it became clear. A woman's leg dangled from the bed. The exposed toes of her left foot touched the floor.

"My God," Peck whispered to himself.

Peck returned to the snowmobile where he tried for twenty minutes before reaching Bender on the walkie-talkie.

"Get back to the office and try to reach the paper company

on the shortwave. Tell them we need a logging rig at a mobile home on Fire Road 99. A tree came down last night. Over."

"Dave, was anybody hurt? Over," Bender said.

Peck hesitated for a moment, lowering the radio.

"Was anybody hurt? Over," Bender said.

Peck raised the radio to his lips. "Yes."

Peck, Bender, McCoy, Kranston and Father Regan stood under the safety of a large pine tree and watched the logging crew prepare a rig to remove the tree from the mobile home.

Peck lit a cigarette and watched a crew supervisor give orders to his men. "Does anybody know this woman?" Peck said.

Kranston said, "Tax records show a Doris White. I can't say I know or remember the woman." He added a fresh stick of gum to the piece he was already chewing.

"Hospital records indicate she had a flu shot last November," McCoy said. "But I administered so many shots that month; I can't say I specifically remember a Doris White."

Peck looked at Regan. "Father?"

The priest nodded. "She was a standard at Sunday mass." Regan turned to make eye contact with Peck. "Her husband died several years ago before you arrived. A logging accident. She was a good woman."

Peck stared at the trailer as he puffed on the cigarette. The rig was in place and the supervisor approached him. "Sheriff, we're ready. It will only take a minute."

Peck nodded and the supervisor gave the order. The rig lifted the massive pine tree and slowly set it on the bay of a logging truck. The supervisor looked at Peck and gave him the all clear sign. Peck tugged at Bender's jacket.

Peck and Bender approached what was left of the front door. Cautiously, they entered the home with flashlights drawn. Peck entered the bedroom first and was completely unprepared for the horrific sight which greeted him.

Tied spread-eagle to the bed with rope, the plump, nude body of Doris White had at least a dozen knife wounds in her chest. Deep, red impressions were on both sides of her neck. Her lifeless eyes were open and stared blankly at the wall.

Peck staggered backward until he hit the wall. "Bender," he shouted. "Jay, get in here."

Bender rushed in and stood next to Peck. He looked at the body of Doris White and shook his head. "She never felt a thing when that tree fell on her."

"Go get the doctor."

Bender nodded and turned away.

"And only the doctor," Peck added.

While Bender went for McCoy, Peck lit a cigarette. He heard McCoy enter the trailer and he called out. "In here."

McCoy entered the bedroom and stood next to Peck. The doctor sighed loudly to himself. "My God, this poor woman."

Peck inhaled on the cigarette and blew out smoke, looking at McCoy. "Examine her, and then tell me was she strangled first, or stabbed?" Peck said.

Peck, Bender, Kranston and Father Regan sat in the van provided by the logging company and waited for McCoy to finish his examination. It was four-thirty in the afternoon and already dark when McCoy exited the trailer and slowly made his way to the van.

In the backseat, Bender slid the door open to allow McCoy to enter. The doctor shook ice from his hat before speaking. "I have to get her to the hospital for a more thorough examination, but my first impression is that she was stabbed to death before he strangled her."

Kranston ran his fingers through his thinning hair. "Who would do such a thing and why?" His voice cracked with stress.

McCoy looked at Peck. "There's more," he said, softly. "She was raped."

Father Regan sighed a deep, anguished sigh at McCoy's words.

Kranston turned away. "I can't listen to this."

Regan leaned forward from the backseat and touched Peck's arm. "I would like to administer last rites."

Peck nodded. "I'll go with you, Father. It isn't pretty."

Peck and Regan left the van, walked to the trailer, and entered. The priest appeared hesitant to walk beyond the remains of the kitchen. Peck gently touched him on the shoulder. "It's okay if you want to turn back," Peck said.

The priest shook his head. "No, I just need a moment."

Gathering his strength, Regan cautiously entered the bedroom where he gasped loudly at the sight of Doris White. "My God in heaven," he whispered.

Peck stood behind the priest, waited and watched.

Regan removed a bible, rosary beads and a sacred vestment from his jacket pocket. He placed the vestment around his neck, opened the Bible and began to pray.

While the priest administered last rites to the body of Doris White, Peck entered the kitchen and used his flashlight to look around. The room was a mess, an absolute disaster. Damage from the tree had crushed or thrown everything in it to the floor.

As Peck rummaged through the rubble, Regan appeared in the doorway.

"I've finished," Regan said. "May God rest and keep her soul."

"Ask Bender to step in here," Peck said. "Then take the van back to town. People at the church will need you. And don't say anything to anybody just yet."

The priest nodded to Peck, turned and slowly exited the trailer.

Peck was turning the small kitchen table right side up when Bender appeared in the doorway. "They're leaving," Bender said.

"We'll take our snowmobiles back to town," Peck said. "Right now, I want to search this place. Leave nothing unturned."

"Leave nothing unturned? Dave, the whole fucking house fell down."

Peck gave Bender an unsympathetic look and the deputy nodded his head.

"You take the kitchen," Peck said.

"Right," Bender said, shining his flashlight around the rubble.

Peck entered the bedroom and shone his flashlight on the floor and walls. The room was such a mess, it would be next to impossible to find any clues or evidence of use. He ran the flashlight across the body of Doris White, searching for something, anything that would provide a clue.

There was nothing.

He was not the FBI, not by a long shot, Peck admitted to himself. He could search the house for a month and not accomplish what an FBI forensics team could in a single day.

Then he noticed a set of pajamas on the floor, tucked under the bed. He reached for them. They were button-top flannels. There was not a tear or a drop of blood on them. In fact, there was not anything to indicate Doris White ever put them on. So why hide them under the bed?

Had she removed them willingly? That was a possibility, though remote. He made her strip for him so he could watch was the more likely scenario.

From the kitchen, Bender called out to him. "Dave, found something."

Peck rushed to the kitchen where Bender was squatting down

over a pile of rubble. In Bender's hand was a large, bloody kitchen knife, part of a set.

"At least we know he didn't bring his own knife to the party," Bender said.

In the hospital lounge, Peck held a meeting with Kranston, McCoy and Bender. A fresh pot of coffee rested centered on the table. Peck poured a cup, lit a cigarette and spoke first.

"Tom, a body will last how long in your freezer?"

"Indefinitely. Even running the generator at intervals, it won't thaw much. It will keep until the state police can move it for autopsy."

Peck looked at Kranston. "Have you reached the state police?"

Kranston's eyes shifted to McCoy before he settled on Peck and finally answered. "They said it would be at least a week before they can send a man. They're stretched pretty thin."

Peck nodded, understanding that the two-hundred-mile trip from Augusta was impossible until the storm finally broke.

"There's something else," Kranston said. He looked at McCoy. "The doctor and I have been talking and we agree that it's best not to inform the town about this incident . . . just yet."

Peck was incredulous. "Not inform the town?"

"At least until the state police arrive."

"We're not talking about portable toilets here, Ed. We're talking about a murdered woman."

"No. We're talking about preventing a widespread panic by hundreds of people forced to live in close quarters as it is," Kranston said.

"We don't want people in the church or hospital thinking the guy next to them is a murderer," McCoy said. "It could start a riot."

"What if the guy next to them *is* a murderer?" Peck said. "Don't they have the right to know that?"

Kranston folded his hands on the table and spoke softly to Peck. "I understand how you feel, Dave. All those years as a homicide cop, it is hard to sit back and do nothing. However, for all we know the man responsible is a drifter. A bum who could be two counties over by now."

"You believe that?" Peck said.

"I don't disbelieve it," Kranston argued.

Peck took a sip of coffee and puffed on his cigarette before answering. "Look, Ed. We know from Tom's examination that Doris White has only been dead less than eighteen hours. In this storm, how far do you think the murderer has gotten?"

"I don't know, Dave," Kranston said. "And neither do you."

McCoy looked at Peck. "It benefits no one to cause a widespread panic."

"It benefits the next victim," Peck said.

"You don't know that there will be a next victim," Kranston said, raising his voice.

"And you don't know that there won't be," Peck said calmly.

Kranston sat back in his chair and the heat seemed to melt out of him. He paused to fish out a stick of gum and when he spoke, it was in a softer, less angry tone of voice. "Once the storm has broken and people are back in their homes, they will less likely panic at the news. A week is not going to matter much considering we do not have the equipment Augusta has. Will it?"

Peck turned to Bender. "You haven't said anything, Jay. What do you think?"

Bender shrugged his shoulders at Peck. "I've known these people a lot longer than you, Dave. Ed is right when he says they will panic. Seeing as how we don't have anything to do anything with . . ." Bender paused to shrug his shoulders again. "And it won't matter much to Doris White one way or the other."

Peck looked at Kranston. "We'll do it your way, Ed. Just so long as you don't object to me quietly poking around on my own."

Kranston nodded. "Quietly."

Peck stood up and left the lounge. Bender glanced at McCoy and Kranston, and then followed Peck outside.

Peck and Bender entered Deb's Diner just after sunrise. There was just one free table by the window. They took a seat and were surprised when Deb arrived to pour them coffee.

"Don't you two look like something the cat dragged in," Deb commented.

"It was a long night," Peck said. "You sleep over?"

"I stayed over, but who could sleep with trees falling every fifteen minutes," Deb said.

"Can I get some eggs?" Bender asked.

"Today, you can. Tomorrow, I would say probably not."

"Are supplies that low?" Peck said.

"You'd be amazed at how much people can eat when they think it's free."

"What else you got?" Peck said.

"Oatmeal, toast, juice, muffins and not much else."

"I guess oatmeal it is," Peck said, looking at Bender.

"I hate oatmeal," Bender said, but sadly nodded his agreement.

Deb walked away and Bender shook his head. "We're not going to make it. Not unless we get a delivery of food."

"That isn't going to happen. Not for at least another week."

"Talk about a panic," Bender said. "You ain't seen nothing until you've seen a Maine hick with an empty stomach and no liquor to drink."

"Hey," Peck said. "I seem to remember you went deer hunting last November."

"Oh, no," Bender said. "I have twelve steaks left in my freezer and I ain't parting with them unless . . ."

"I don't mean that," Peck said.

"What then?"

"Half the men in this town just love to go shooting things in the woods. Talk to your hunting buddies and see who would be willing to go out hunting. Deer, wild turkey, whatever is around you can shoot. I'd bet they'd love the chance to do some poaching."

Bender smiled. "Son of a bitch, I want to be just like Dave when I grow up."

Deb returned with two large bowls of oatmeal. "I doubt you'll ever grow up, Jay." She set the bowls on the table. "It isn't good, but it will fill your stomach."

Bender shook his head, picked up the sugar bowl, and tossed several spoonfuls onto the oatmeal. He added four pats of butter, then stirred it up and took a quick taste. Not satisfied, he reached for the bottle of maple syrup and added an ounce to the mixture, then tried it again. "Better."

"For God's sake," Deb said and turned away.

Bender looked at Peck. "What?"

Peck tried his oatmeal. It was bland, but as Deb said, it would fill his stomach.

"Are we going back out today?" Bender said as he spooned maple-colored oatmeal into his mouth.

Peck shook his head. "People are sleeping in shifts as it is. The church and hospital can't hold any more."

Bender ate some more, then looked at Peck and smiled. "They don't have to."

"They don't have to what?"

"Sleep in shifts."

"Why?"

"Before I became your deputy, you remember I worked for

the paper company. They have an old logging camp about seven miles west of Main Street off a dirt road. It's been abandoned since Korea."

"What's there?"

"A dozen cabins, a main hall, it will hold forty-eight people."

"Any generators?"

Bender shook his head. "No, but there's a woodstove in each cabin and a large fireplace in the main hall."

"It's not on the map."

"That map is new. It's been closed seven years now."

"Check it out. If it's safe, we'll use it."

Deb returned with a fresh pot of coffee. "I sent Paco home to get some sleep."

"You want a ride to your house?" Peck said.

"Later, maybe. Around six if I can get away."

Peck nodded. "If I'm asleep, wake me up."

Bender ate another spoonful of oatmeal and looked at Deb. "Maybe I can get some toast?"

Peck lay on the cot in his office and listened to the mixture of sounds of wind and the ice plinking against the window against the backdrop of a soft crackle from the woodstove. Except for the faint light escaping from the woodstove, the room was completely dark.

Exhausted, sleep came easy and he drifted off in a matter of minutes.

An hour or so later, Peck opened his eyes when a headache radiated across his forehead and settled between his eyes. He stood up from the cot and lit a candle on his desk for light. Opening a desk drawer, Peck found a bottle of aspirin and poured three tablets into his hand. He crossed the room to the water cooler, filled a paper cup and swallowed the three aspirins in one gulp.

Turning toward the cot, Peck took several steps when a bolt of lightning struck him between the eyes. Stunned, Peck froze in his tracks, and then dropped to one knee and gasped for air. Momentarily, his vision dimmed.

As quickly as the pain struck, it vanished.

Peck stood up, walked several more steps, dropped to the floor when the pain struck a second time, rolled to his side, and gasped for air. He ripped at his T-shirt as the searing, white heat inside his head all but blinded him.

Then, seconds later, the pain was completely gone. His vision returned to normal and his breathing was fine.

Slowly, Peck worked his way to one knee before he finally stood up and tested his legs. He went to his desk, opened the drawer, poured two fingers of scotch into a plastic cup, and downed it in two swallows. The liquor went down hard and radiated heat in his stomach.

As the lone candle flickered, casting an eerie, yellow light across the desk, Peck wiped sweat from his face and stared at the tiny flame. Never in his life had he experienced such a headache. Maybe it was the dry air from the constant use of the woodstove, which dried out his sinuses and triggered the attack.

Whatever the cause, the pain was gone. Peck stood up and cracked the window to allow fresh air to circulate in the room, and then returned to the cot. Before he fell asleep, he made a mental note to see Doctor McCoy for something stronger than aspirin.

When Peck woke for the second time that day, it was already dark outside the office window. He dressed quickly, went outside and crossed the street to the hospital. He found McCoy in the lounge where a fresh pot of coffee rested on a burner.

"I want a coffee, a cigarette and a hot shower," Peck told McCoy.

"Sure," McCoy said. "The generator's on, the water's hot."

"And after that, I want a checkup."

"A checkup? What for?"

Peck filled a mug with coffee, and then looked at McCoy. "A headache."

Shirtless after his first shower in days, Peck sat on the edge of an examination table and watched McCoy scribble notes on a chart. "And just like that the pain went away?" McCoy said, glancing at Peck.

"Just like that, gone. What do you think?"

"Your blood pressure is 120 over 70. It doesn't get much better than that without being dead," McCoy said. "Resting pulse is 80, lungs are clear, eyes are tip-top."

"I didn't imagine being knocked on my ass, Tom."

"I didn't say you did," McCoy said setting the chart aside. "Exhaustion, too much coffee, too much stress, lack of sleep, pick one, pick them all and you've got a migraine."

Peck reached for his shirt and slipped it on. "I thought migraines lasted for hours."

"Not necessarily. Not if it's what is known as a cluster headache," McCoy said. "They strike suddenly, knock you for a loop, and vanish just as suddenly. They come and go in bunches, or clusters. They can last seconds, minutes or hours. They can be brutal."

"Why all of a sudden?"

"Who says that it is? They could have been brewing below the surface for years and decided now was the right time to take a peek at the world," McCoy said. "Or it could just be an isolated incident from dry sinus passages. Either way, I can't find a damn thing wrong with you."

Peck tucked his shirt into his pants and looked at McCoy.

"Anything you can give me? For next time, if there is a next time."

McCoy looked at Peck and hesitated several seconds before he answered. "Sure, but only use it if you have another headache. Okay?"

Peck nodded. "What else would I do with it?"

"And get some moisture in the office," McCoy said. "Put a pot of water on the woodstove like in the old days."

Peck adjusted his utility belt, feeling the weight of his heavy revolver on his right hip. "Anything else?"

"Yeah, come into my office. I keep the good stuff locked up," McCoy said. "Then, let's get something to eat. Sometimes an empty stomach can cause severe headaches."

Deb was behind the counter when Peck and McCoy entered the diner. It was another full house, but they managed to grab a table vacated by two of her waitresses returning from break.

Deb approached the table with a pot of coffee. "Paco's working the night shift, Sheriff. I'd appreciate that ride home and so would my feet."

Peck held out his coffee cup while Deb poured. "The ice seems to be letting up a bit. It should be no problem."

"Good. What will you have?"

"What are our choices?" McCoy asked.

"Fried chicken with mashed potatoes."

"Or?" McCoy said.

"Fried chicken with mashed potatoes."

Peck took a sip of his coffee. "I guess I'll have that."

McCoy shrugged. "Me, too."

Peck glided the snowmobile to a gentle stop directly in front of the stairs that led to Deb Robertson's front door. She climbed off and looked at her dark house. "It must be freezing in there," she said. "Maybe you could help me build a fire?"

Peck looked at the pitch-black windows and immediately thought of Doris White. "All right," he said.

They climbed the stairs and Deb unlocked her door with a key. They stepped inside and the temperature wasn't much warmer than outside, maybe in the low forties.

"Start on the fire," Deb said. "I'm going to crank the generator before icicles start growing off the ceiling."

Peck used his flashlight to guide them across the living room where Deb lit several candles on the coffee table. She took hold of Peck's flashlight. "I'll be right back," she said.

There was a firewood box near the woodstove. Peck loaded the stove with kindling from the box and ignited it with a foot-long match and old newspapers. As the kindling took hold, Peck heard the hum of the generator in the background.

Deb appeared in the doorway of the living room. "There. It will only take a few minutes for the heat to come on. Feel like some fresh coffee?"

"That sounds good," Peck said as he toyed with the kindling.

Deb smiled at him and entered the kitchen. At fifty-three, the schoolboy jitters he felt at being alone with an attractive woman should have left him long ago, but they hadn't. In the back of his mind, Peck felt that something besides the woodstove was heating up inside the house.

When the kindling was burning hot enough, Peck added a few heavy logs. In a matter of minutes, the fire was roaring, warming the entire room.

Deb entered with a serving tray of coffee and cups. She lowered the tray to the coffee table and poured two cups, then took a seat on the sofa. Peck walked to the sofa, sat down and picked up his cup. Deb looked at him.

"You're a mysterious man, Sheriff," Deb said.

"In what way?"

"You've been here eighteen months and hardly anyone knows anything about you. Why is that?"

"There's nothing to know," Peck said, sipping from the cup. "I'm a pretty boring, middle-aged guy with nothing to tell."

"Then you won't mind me being nosy and asking some questions."

"Like?"

"What's it like to live in a big city like Baltimore?"

Peck took another sip of coffee. "Like living anywhere else, I suppose. It's just bigger with more people around to bother you and get in your way while you try to protect them."

"No big-city stories? No modern museums or theaters?" She raised an eyebrow at him that was very sexy to watch. "All those big plays and shows."

Peck shrugged. "You don't attend many theaters and shows on a cop's pay. Besides, I never was the theater-going type."

Deb smiled and shook her head. "Women, girlfriends, wives?"

Peck stared at her in such a way, Deb blushed along the base of her neck to her cheeks. Peck found that very sexy, too.

"I'm sorry, Dave. That was a terrible question," Deb said.

Peck shook his head. "Not at all. It's not the question, but the answer. I've never been married. Never even been close."

"That is really surprising. You're a very attractive man."

Peck didn't know what to make of that comment. Maybe there was nothing to make. She could be engaging in simple conversation based on what she said, being nosy. "Not really. I was a cop for twenty-seven years. There wasn't a whole lot of time for dating and looking for the right woman. After a while, it didn't seem to matter all that much."

Deb nodded in such a way that it told him she understood. "I was married," she confessed. "He died fifteen years ago when I was only thirty."

"I'm sorry."

"Don't be. It was along time ago and I'm over it and moved on."

There was an uncomfortable moment of silence and Peck used the time to sip coffee. Deb smiled at him and stood up. "I'll be right back," she said.

"I'm going to have to get going," Peck said. "I have things I need to do."

Deb reached down to silence him with a finger to his lips. "I'll be right back. Don't move, okay? There's nothing that important back at the office it can't wait a few more minutes."

Peck met her eyes and felt himself nod and she turned and left the living room. Peck looked at the fire in the woodstove and lit a cigarette. He wasn't sure what the point was behind Deb's line of questioning, other than curiosity. Maybe he had been a bit standoffish since he arrived, but old, city habits are hard to shake once they take root. When things settled down, after the storm broke and the state police arrived to investigate the murder, he would make a conscious effort to open up a bit more. In the meantime, he became aware of the sweat building up on the palms of his hands and a slight queasiness in his stomach. He wiped them on his pants, feeling silly, like a nervous kid.

There was a noise and Peck turned his head to look at Deb, who was standing in the doorway of the living room. She had changed into a white, full-length, silk robe and nothing else. She took several steps forward and candlelight behind her shone through the robe, exposing all the curves and mounds of her body. Not that it mattered because parted down the middle, the open robe did little to hide the tips of her breasts and triangle of pubic hair.

"I've tried everything to get your attention, Sheriff. Nothing seems to work," Deb said as she walked toward him. "What does it take?"

She stopped at the sofa and looked at him with her gray, sensuous eyes.

Peck stared at her breasts and the triangular patch of dark hair. Her stomach was rigid and flat and showed no sign of her forty-five years. The nipples on her breasts were firm and defied her age as well. She was a remarkable-looking woman. "That," he whispered, not knowing why he said it or what else to say.

"Now be a good law enforcement agent and come over here," Deb said and yanked him to his feet.

She kissed him full on the lips, and then broke apart when Peck didn't respond. "What's wrong?"

Peck smiled weakly. "Nothing is wrong. I just can't remember the last time I kissed a woman."

Deb's face registered her surprise. "Sheriff, there is more to life than catching bad guys and writing parking tickets."

She reached for Peck's heavy utility belt, unhooked it and it fell to the floor. "Here is an example," she said and opened his pants and pushed him to the sofa.

Heat was the only word that came to mind to describe the sensation he felt in his loins when Deb gently touched him. It made him uncomfortable, like a kid on his first date. He tried to stand, but she pushed him back against the sofa and removed his heavy boots.

"Deb, I don't know . . ."

She covered his mouth with her hand. "Just be quiet," she whispered as she stripped him of his pants. "I don't often get the chance to do something like this."

Peck gasped when she took him in her mouth. Her eyes looked up at him and seemed to smile at his near immediate response.

The first time they made love on the sofa, Peck was like a runaway freight train. It was quick and clumsy and over in a matter of minutes. She toyed with his hair and told him it was all right, that practice makes perfect.

The second time was in the bedroom. She aroused him slowly using her mouth and hands and he responded, much to his surprise, like a man twenty years younger. They came together and he knew that he pleased her because after thirty minutes, she dug her nails into his back and drew tiny beads of blood.

Afterward, they caught their breath and stretched out on the bed. "See, practice is the key, Dave. Maybe you better come around more often."

They fell asleep for several hours, curled up against each other.

Peck stirred and finally awoke. Deb had shifted in her sleep and her head rested against his chest. He gently lifted her and rolled out of the bed, careful not to disturb her. Then he went downstairs to find his cigarettes and lit one. Walking to the window, he looked out.

The storm had mostly passed; the hail was little more than a fine mist of ice particles. In the background, thunder rumbled low in the sky. Snow lightning flashed and for a split second, it was broad daylight outside the window. Then the sky darkened and thunder rumbled once again.

Seemingly captivated, Peck continued to stare out the window. Lightning flashed and bolted to the ground and thunder boomed, echoing for several seconds.

A thought entered into his mind. He honestly could not remember the name of the last woman he slept with, it was so long ago. He could see her face as a dim shadow. She had shoulder-length blond hair, with pale skin and blue eyes. Her name suited her looks, but nothing familiar popped into his mind no matter how hard he tried to place it.

Did it matter?

Deb was right; there was more to life than parking tickets. Much more.

The lightning flashed again, several times in quick succession. As thunder cracked loudly, Peck felt a tiny speck of pain between his eyes. He rubbed the spot with his fingers until it went away.

Peck returned to the bedroom, slipped between the covers, and felt the warmth of Deb's body against his. Listening to her shallow breathing, he was lulled back to sleep. When they both awoke, it was early into the next morning. Wrapped in each other's arms, they greeted the new day with a smile.

Driving the snowmobile back to the center of town, Peck relived the events of the morning in his mind. He made a fire while the generator heated the water hot enough for them to share a bath together. He shaved using one of her razors. In the tub, they made love for the third time in a span of twelve hours. To his surprise and her delight, arousal was almost instantaneous and the event lasted nearly thirty minutes.

Afterward, while he dressed, Deb fixed a hot breakfast. They parted with a kiss at the door. He told her he would see her later on if he could get away. She told him busy or not, a warm bed and a hot meal beat the hell out of a cold cot and a woodstove in the office. He had to admit that she was right.

Halfway to town, the hail finally let up. The sun shown for the first time in days and light glistened off the ice-covered branches of the trees like sparkling diamonds. He stopped along a trail to admire the shining star of nature and smoke a cigarette.

By the time he arrived at the office, it was just after ten a.m. Bender and Kranston were huddled around the shortwave, listening to a weather update from Augusta. The news was fairly good.

"Well, good morning, Sheriff," Kranston said when Peck entered the office.

Bender grinned at him as he removed his jacket and tossed it on the coat rack. "What?" Peck said to his deputy.

Kranston switched off the shortwave. "Ten days to two weeks before power is fully restored, so they say. We'd be lucky to see a month. But at least the ice has let up statewide."

Peck lifted the coffee pot from the woodstove and poured a cup, then sat behind his desk. "How is our food supply?"

Kranston took the chair opposite Peck's desk. "Genius, Dave. Bender and his hunting buddies bagged two deer, a half dozen wild turkeys and who knows how many snow shoe hares?"

"Fifteen," Bender said.

"The deer have been stripped, a couple of turkeys are already in the oven and Deb has promised to make stew from the rabbits," Kranston said.

"She did? When did you talk to her?"

Bender suddenly stood up from his desk. "I think it's safe to take the cruiser out for a drive. I'm going to take a spin around and see if we got any stragglers who need a ride."

"Throw a gas can in the trunk," Peck said. "And take your radio."

Bender left the office and Peck looked at Kranston. "About the other day, I shouldn't have lost my temper. We're paying you to enforce the law and you were just doing your job."

Peck accepted Kranston's feeble attempt at an apology. "Any talk?"

Kranston shook his head. "Why would there be? Nobody except us knows of the incident."

"What about the state police?"

Again, Kranston shook his head. "Not yet, maybe tomorrow."

"You said you spoke to Deb Robertson," Peck said. "Did you mean this morning?"

Kranston looked at Peck and there was a brief pause before he answered. "I'm losing track of time, I suppose. It was probably yesterday."

Peck stood up from his desk. "In that case, I think I'll see if I can catch Jay."

Kranston remained motionless as Peck reached for his coat and left the office. After he was gone, Kranston sat motionless for several minutes before he stood up and looked out the window. Removing a pack of gum from a pocket, he slipped a stick out of its wrapper and placed it in his mouth.

Bender was inspecting the heavy chains on the tires of the cruiser when Peck entered the underground garage. Bender didn't look happy.

"We need a new car, Dave. This '53 won't last another winter," Bender said.

"She'll make it to summer when the '60 models come out."

"Yeah, we got one in the budget?"

"No."

"Want to drive?"

"No."

Bender opened his door and got behind the wheel. Peck entered the passenger side. Bender started the engine and the heavy cruiser clanged loudly as he rolled it up the exit ramp.

"Tell Kranston we at least want it in the budget to get a radio like the big city cops have," Bender said. "This hand-held junk don't cut it."

Peck lit a cigarette and turned his head to look at Bender. "Who else do we have to call but each other?"

"There," Bender said and pointed to a spot past the steering wheel of the cruiser.

Off in the distance about a hundred yards down the dirt road Bender had turned onto was the abandoned logging camp. Bender turned onto a plowed driveway and slowed the heavy cruiser to a stop in front of the main cabin. "I asked them to plow," Bender said. "They must have come by yesterday."

"Who, the paper company?" Peck said.

Bender nodded. "It's still their property." They exited and walked to the front door of the main facility, which was a log cabin about sixty-by-sixty in size. Peck tried the doorknob and looked at Bender.

"It's open."

"I told them we might want to use it."

They entered the large, rustic hall, which looked more like a hunting lodge than a logging camp. The air smelled damp and musty. Peck scanned the interior, noting the two fireplaces, tables, chairs, sofas and pool tables, all generic in appearance and a decade out of date in style.

"It isn't wired for electricity, but they got it set up for generators, lights and cooking," Bender said.

"You stayed here?"

Bender nodded. "I was maybe twenty-one, right before they closed it down. Logging is back-breaking work."

"It will do," Peck said. "We'll tell Ed when we get back to town."

"Feel like looking for some stragglers now?" Bender said.

"Yes."

"Want to drive?"

"No."

It was after six p.m. when Peck and Bender returned to the center of town. Their first stop was Deb's Diner where it was another full house. After a fifteen minute wait, one of Deb's waitresses led them to a window table where Doctor McCoy and Father Regan joined them.

As the waitress poured coffee, Peck looked at her. "Is Deb around?"

"Not yet. Paco swung by her place on the way in earlier. She said she would drive herself now that the ice has stopped."

Peck nodded and the waitress took their orders.

"I can't say I like the idea of her driving herself," Regan said.

"She has that big ole truck," Bender said, looking at Peck. "A brand new Ford with snow tires and chains."

Peck ignored Bender's comment and looked at McCoy. "Anybody get wind of Doris White?"

"Not that I could determine. If they have, nobody said anything to me."

"Somebody must know her. You're sure nobody's asked or missed her?" Peck said.

McCoy shook his head. "Not to me."

Regan said, "By my count, we have two hundred town residents staying at the church and hospital. That leaves a hundred or so still in their homes. People must figure she is one of those hundred, if they figure anything at all."

"What about Sunday mass?" Peck said.

"What about it?" Regan sipped coffee, looking at Peck over the rim of the cup.

"You said she was a regular at Sunday mass," Peck said. "Sunday is two days from now. Somebody might notice she isn't there and ask around. Maybe take a ride out to her place to check on her. They come back and ask questions, then what?"

Regan's surprise registered in his eyes. "I . . . hadn't thought of that."

Bender said, "We might have the state police here by then. I wouldn't worry too much about it until we have to."

Peck sipped coffee and looked at Bender. "Jay, rule number one in a homicide investigation is you never stop worrying until the jury says guilty."

With a crackling fire for background noise, Bender twisted frequency knobs on the shortwave radio. After several minutes of static, he shut it off and looked at Peck who was at his desk, making notes.

"Nothing," Bender said. "You think somebody would be there. Anybody."

Peck looked up from his notes. "A few hundred state cops scattered throughout a state the size of Maine, what makes you think they're sitting around waiting for a distress call from us?"

Frustrated, Bender slapped the side of the shortwave radio on his way to his desk. "And where the hell is Kranston?"

"Home and asleep in his own bed if he has any sense."

Bender checked his watch and looked at Peck. "It's after eleven. I think I'll go home and try to get some sleep."

Peck scribbled a note. "No reason for the both of us to lose a night's sleep." The truth was he could hardly wait to see Deb again and hoped Bender's interest in the state police would wane and he would do what he said and go home.

Bender stood up and reached for his jacket on the coat hook when the door opened and one of Deb's waitresses entered the office.

"Sheriff, Jay, can I see you for a minute?" she said.

Peck and Bender looked at her. She appeared nervous and her eyes darted back and forth between the two men.

"Yes?" Peck said. "Is there something we can help you with?"

"She didn't come in. I thought I should tell you."

"Who, you mean Deb?" Peck said.

The waitress nodded. "It's probably nothing, but we asked Paco to take a run to her place on his way home and check on her. It's silly, but . . ."

"No," Peck said. "It isn't."

"So much for going home," Bender said. He looked at Peck. "I'll go warm up the car."

Peck nodded to Bender, and then looked at the waitress. "Are you off work?"

"Yes."

"Can you get home?"

"I have a ride."

"Go home. Stay there. Everything will be fine," Peck said. "And don't worry. Deb probably couldn't get her truck started and there's no phones to call."

The waitress smiled at Peck. "You're probably right. I'm probably worrying for nothing."

"You did the right thing," Peck said. As he stood up, he could feel the anxiety building up in his stomach. "I'll walk you out."

Three

Bender had a steady hand behind the wheel of the heavy cruiser. The drive to Deb Robertson's home took thirty minutes, as Bender had to hold speed to thirty-five miles an hour to avoid severe skid-out on the ice-covered roads.

When they arrived at her home, Bender parked the cruiser close to Deb's pickup. Peck exited the cruiser first and immediately knew something was wrong when he found the stalled pickup with the gearshift in park.

Bender exited the cruiser and stood next to Peck. "I don't get it. She was warming up her truck and let it stall?"

Peck's eyes went to the house. It was completely dark. Not even a candle was burning. Smoke was not visible from the chimney and the generator was quiet. "I don't think so," he said. A tight ball was forming in his gut.

"Then what?" Bender said, his eyes following Peck's gaze.

"Let's find out what," Peck said.

They walked to the stairs and climbed to the top. Bender peered through a dark window, then shrugged at Peck. "Nothing," Bender said. Peck looked at Bender, then knocked on the door and it slowly swung open.

"Shit," Bender whispered.

Peck pulled the flashlight from his belt and Bender did the same. Peck stepped inside, followed by Bender.

"It's freezing in here," Bender whispered, able to see his own breath.

"Take the first floor," Peck said. "Yell if you find anything."

Bender nodded and moved toward the kitchen. Peck walked to the stairs and climbed to the second floor. "Deb, it's Dave. Are you in here?"

Peck's request went unanswered. He reached the second floor where he paused for a moment to scan the flashlight around the hallway. At the top of the landing, against the wall, Peck remembered a small table where a second phone rested. The table was sideways on the floor. The phone was halfway across the hallway.

Peck shifted the flashlight to his left hand and drew his revolver. He approached the master bedroom where the door was halfway open. "Deb, are you in there?"

The silence was unsettling as Peck pushed the bedroom door completely open. Entering the bedroom, Peck swung the flashlight around the room, where end tables were overturned. A wood chair was broken and clothing littered the floor.

Peck aimed the flashlight on the bed. He dropped the flashlight and revolver to the floor and grabbed his head in his hands. The room was suddenly spinning around him. "Oh God . . . oh no . . . oh God . . . oh no," he screamed.

Bender was suddenly in the bedroom, breathing hard from running. "Dave, what is . . . Jesus Mary, mother of God."

With the hum of the generator as background noise, Peck, Kranston, Bender and Father Regan sat at the kitchen table and drank coffee, while they waited for Doctor McCoy to complete his examination. McCoy had been at it for nearly thirty minutes and that span of time seemed an endless eternity. Every so often, they could hear a creak in a floorboard as McCoy walked around the master bedroom. The sound was unnerving.

Peck lit a cigarette, his fourth in a row, and then took a sip of coffee.

Kranston cleared his throat as he looked at Peck. "Dave, I . . . don't know what to say. You were right all along. I can't believe this has happened. I've known Deb . . . I can't believe this has happened."

Peck remained silent and took another sip of coffee. Above his head, the floorboard creaked.

Regan removed rosary beads from a pocket and clutched them tightly between his fingers. Peck glanced at the priest and saw Regan's lips move in silent prayer.

Peck turned to Bender. "When you went for McCoy, did you try the state police like I asked you to?"

"For a half hour," Bender said. "All I could raise was static."

"Try again when we get back."

Bender nodded his head. "The roads are drivable. I could try making the trip."

"If we get no response," Peck agreed.

Kranston looked at Peck. "I take responsibility for this, Dave. If I hadn't been so stubborn about making the news public, Deb would still be alive."

Peck shook his head. "You don't know that. Nobody does. The man who killed her is responsible and only that man."

"If I listened to you, if we warned people of . . ."

McCoy's footsteps drew their attention and all heads turned to the staircase. McCoy descended and walked to the kitchen table. His face was ashen, drained of any color and appeared to have aged ten years. He quietly sat down next to Peck.

"Doctor?" Peck said when McCoy remained quiet.

"You were right, Dave. I'm sorry," McCoy said. "This should not have happened. It was preventable." He looked at Peck. "We should have listened to you."

"It was the same man, wasn't it?" Peck said.

"I'm a country doctor, Dave."

"But you are a doctor."

"Yes, I am a doctor, which doesn't qualify me as a forensics expert."

"But as a doctor," Peck insisted.

McCoy looked at Peck. "There is little doubt that both women were killed by the same man. The angle of the stab wounds, the knots in the ropes."

"Thank you," Peck said. He looked at Father Regan. "If you're ready, I'll walk up with you, Father."

The priest looked at Peck through red eyes filled with pain, and then stood up.

Peck stood up and joined Regan. Together, they slowly ascended the stairs to the second floor. At the bedroom, Regan cautiously entered, then made a sound that could only be described as anguish at the sight of Deb Robertson's body.

In a fashion similar to Doris White, Deb Robertson was spread-eagle on the bed, bound to the bedposts with rope. A dozen knife wounds were visible in her chest. Red impressions on her neck were so deep finger markings were visible. Dried blood stained the sheets and the floor near the bed and appeared quite black.

Regan turned to Peck and tears filled the priest's eyes. "How can people do this to other people? Why?"

Peck did not respond and watched Regan as the priest moved to the bed where he began to recite the sacrament of last rites.

Peck watched the priest for as long as he could stand it, then turned away and waited in the hallway. Regan began to pray, first in English and then in Latin. Peck closed his eyes and tried to drown out the priest's voice.

Seated on the sofa in the living room, Regan openly wept into his hands. Peck placed a hand on his shoulder and gave him a reassuring, gentle squeeze before he went to the kitchen and looked at Jay. "Take everybody back, then put chains on the ambulance and return with the doctor."

"That could take a while," Bender said. "A couple of hours."

Peck looked at Bender. "She isn't going anywhere."

Alone on the sofa, the house was cold and silent. The generator had run out of gas and candles burned for light. For something to do, Peck went around back, filled the generator from a gas can and pulled the start cord. The generator fired to life. He stood there for several minutes, staring at the generator, listening to its deafening, gas-powered engine, delaying the inevitable of reentering the house.

Finally returning to the living room, Peck clicked on the lights. On the sofa was a large, black carrying case. Picking up the case, Peck went upstairs to the master bedroom where he set the case aside and slipped on a pair of rubber gloves.

Walking slowly, Peck did a visual inspection of every item in the room. An upturned rocking chair was on the floor near the foot of the bed. The night before, when he stayed over, the rocker had been in the corner of the room against the wall. A teddy bear rested on its seat. Peck found it under the bed, soaked in blood.

Someone, the killer probably, had moved the chair. With Deb tied up and helpless, the sick son of a bitch took a comfortable spot in the rocker where he had a bird's-eye view of his demented handiwork.

Women's pajamas and Deb's robe lay tossed across the dresser. Peck inspected them and could find no traces of blood. Not even a small tear. Had the killer made her strip for him like he probably made Doris White?

It was possible she knew him and even invited him unknowingly to her bedroom. Was her murderer another lover? It was a thought Peck did not want to face, though he knew that he had to as part of the investigation.

Peck stopped at the bed and stared for many long minutes at the lifeless body. The killer used everyday, common rope which was available anywhere. Did he bring his own or find it in the house?

The multiple stab wounds came from a kitchen bread knife and were similar to the wounds in Doris White's chest. Formed by a downward, striking motion, the wounds were deep, some penetrating the breastplate. The weapon was nowhere in the house. He probably took it with him and discarded it deep in the woods or kept it as a trophy, a sick reminder to relive the experience.

Peck noticed something on the fingertips of Deb's right hand. Using a pocketknife, Peck cut the ropes and lifted the hand for a closer look. There were remnants of dried blood under the nails. He would bet the blood was not her own.

Deb had fought her assailant and she died hard.

From what little he knew of her, that seemed to fit her personality. She was not the type to lie down and go out without a fight. Maybe it was that fight which cost her her life. Maybe Doris White, too. Maybe if they had been passive?

Peck righted the rocking chair, sat it in and lit a cigarette. He stared at the lifeless body on the bed as he smoked. If this were Baltimore, a team of detectives would jump on the murders the moment they made a connection between the two women with the idea of a serial killer/rapist case as a ticket to bigger and better things. Nothing motivated homicide detectives like a juicy story above the fold. More often than not, that motivation led to a quick and satisfactory conclusion.

If this were in Baltimore.

In Dunston nowhere Falls, Maine, you sat in a rocking chair and waited for the state police to dig their cars out of the snow and hoped they had chains on their tires. Or you got around by decade-old snowmobiles and hoped they didn't break down.

In the meantime, three hundred innocent people were at the mercy of a very sick and violent man who murdered twice and probably wouldn't stop, not until he was either caught or killed.

Peck stood up and put his cigarette out in the toilet in the bathroom. He picked up the black case, opened it and removed a box camera. He inserted a bulb and took a picture from the foot of the bed. He took another from the left side, then the right. There were three bulbs left in the case. As he removed a spent bulb and reached into the case for a fresh one, the pain in his head struck so unexpectedly and so viciously, he was on the floor without realizing he had fallen.

Holding his head, Peck rolled onto his side into the fetal position. The pounding in his head grew even worse as the pressure behind his eyes amplified. Blood ran down his nose in tiny droplets. He could taste it as it touched his lips, sickly sweet and sticky.

Pushing himself to all fours, Peck attempted to stand, but a fit of dizziness overtook him and he fell face first to the rug with the floor spinning around him.

He closed his eyes and attempted to steady his breathing to keep from passing out. Slowly the spinning sensation waned and his head began to steady. Then, in the darkness behind his eyes, a vision slowly began to form.

A fire burned in yellow and red flames, so vivid in color he felt as if he could reach out and touch them. In the background of Peck's mind, there was an anguished cry for help, shouted barely above a whisper in a child's voice. A small hand, the hand of a child reached out for him, desperate for contact.

On the floor, Peck felt himself reach out with his right hand to try to touch the child's hand he saw in his mind's image. Instinctively, Peck knew the child was in some kind of mortal danger.

As their fingers met, the fire suddenly burst into an uncontrolled wall of searing hot flames. Peck felt a stabbing sensation of pain in his head. An explosion echoed somewhere in the background and the chaotic vision vanished into darkness, leaving Peck breathless and drenched in a cold sweat. He lay still for a minute, trying to breathe and regain control of his muscles.

Then, pushing himself to all fours, Peck slowly crawled toward the bathroom. Gasping for air, he reached the toilet where the bile in his stomach rose up and forced him to vomit until his stomach was empty and the muscles cramped.

Rolling onto his back, Peck looked at the ceiling. "Ah, Jesus, Deb," he said aloud, and then began to weep openly.

Peck loaded the fireplace with wood and built a roaring fire to warm the house. He poured a drink of Deb's expensive scotch at the corner bar, then took a seat on the sofa before the fire. As he smoked a cigarette, he replayed the episode from the bedroom in his mind. Whatever the hell that was, it was no headache and no amount of aspirin was going to fix it. After finishing the scotch, he stretched out on the sofa and exhaustion overtook him.

Peck was asleep on the sofa in the living room when Bender and McCoy entered the house. McCoy touched Peck's shoulder and gently shook him. Peck opened his eyes, sat up and looked at his watch.

"It's five in the morning," Bender said.

"The chains took a while," McCoy explained. "Sorry we were so late getting back."

Bender handed Peck a mug of coffee from the kitchen. "I made it before we woke you up," he said.

"I must have dozed off." Peck took the mug, blew on it a few times and cautiously sipped the steaming hot coffee.

"The ambulance is outside," McCoy said. "Jay and I will

carry out the body, if you'd like?"

Peck nodded and took another sip from the mug.

McCoy and Bender went to the stairs where the doctor picked up a body bag.

Peck lit a cigarette and watched them ascend the stairs to the bedroom. He could hear Jay and McCoy lift the body of Deb Robertson and place her into the bag. There was a moment of silence, followed by the loud zip of the body bag.

As McCoy and Bender carried the lifeless body of Deb Robertson down the stairs and to the front door, Peck stared into the fire and choked back a tear.

In the hospital lounge, McCoy listened carefully as Peck described his nightmarish attack on the floor of Deb Robertson's bedroom. Every few seconds, McCoy scribbled a note on a pad and nodded his head.

When Peck was finished, McCoy stood up. "Let's go out back."

Peck followed McCoy to an examination room. "Take your shirt off and have a seat," McCoy said.

Peck removed his shirt and T-shirt and sat on the examination table. McCoy picked up a small flashlight. "Open your mouth, Dave."

For fifteen minutes, McCoy examined Peck. Blood pressure, heart, pulse rate, ears, nose and throat, reflexes, he checked it all and even felt for tumors.

"Put your shirt on," McCoy said when he was finished.

Peck reached for his T-shirt. "Well?"

"I don't know," McCoy confessed.

"You don't know?"

"I'm a doctor, not a miracle worker, Dave."

"But something must have caused that. I didn't wind up with my head in the toilet for no reason."

"There's a reason," McCoy confessed. "There always is. I just don't know what it is at the moment."

Peck slipped his shirt on and tucked it into his pants.

"Look," McCoy said. "Other than your blood pressure being slightly elevated at the moment, and that's understandable, you're tip-top. I see no cause for alarm, but I'm going to call Maine Medical Center and schedule an appointment with a neurologist."

"A neurologist? Why, what do you think is wrong with me?"

"I don't think anything is wrong with you," McCoy said. "That's the problem."

"What about those pills you gave me?" Peck said.

"I've got something stronger, but I don't want you to take it unless it's absolutely necessary."

Peck allowed himself a tiny smile. "Define necessary."

McCoy responded with a smile of his own. "Your head in the toilet qualifies."

Seated behind his desk, Peck looked at Kranston, who occupied the chair opposite him. Both men were silent, lost in thought. The only noise in the room it seemed was the sound of Kranston's constant gum chewing.

"You look tired, Ed," Peck finally said.

"I am, but not nearly as much as you."

Peck glanced at his watch. "It's four in the afternoon and there's nothing more we can do right now. Why don't you go home?"

"Why don't you?"

Peck stood up from behind the desk, walked to the woodstove and fueled the fire with several heavy logs. He stirred things around with a poker until the logs caught fire.

Returning to his desk, Peck said, "This is home, for now. At least until the state police call us back."

Kranston sighed to himself. "I could use a drink."

Peck opened a desk drawer and produced the bottle of scotch. "One finger or two?"

"Better make it three."

Peck opened the bottle and poured scotch into two plastic cups. "Three it is."

Kranston tossed the gum into the trash can, picked up his cup and took a sip. "I feel rather guilty, sitting here by a warm fire, drinking scotch. Safe, while two women are dead."

"Feeling guilty won't help," Peck said. "It only gets in the way and makes matters worse by fogging your judgment. It is best to keep your mind free of guilt, anger or anything else until he's caught. There's plenty of time afterwards for that."

"That's right," Kranston said, respectfully. "I keep forgetting this isn't your first murder case, is it?"

Peck took a sip of his drink as he looked at Kranston. "A homicide cop always hopes each murder is his last. It never is, though. There's always another just around the bend, waiting to be discovered, hoping to be solved."

Across the room, the shortwave radio suddenly came to life. Static gave way to the voice of Sergeant Goodwin of the Maine State Police.

"This is Sergeant Goodwin of the Maine State Police in Augusta. I am responding to a distress call. Over," Goodwin said.

Peck and Kranston looked at each other, and then ran to Bender's desk where the shortwave radio was located.

Peck picked up the heavy transmitter. "This is Sheriff David Peck of Dunston Falls. We placed the call. Over."

"Sorry about the delay, Sheriff. Power is out statewide and I'm on generator. What is the nature of your distress call? Over."

"Sergeant, I need a forensics team and homicide. I have two murders committed several days apart. Over."

There was a slight pause before Goodwin responded, incredulously. "Two? There was only thirteen in the entire state last year. Over."

"Last year," Peck said. "How soon can you send somebody? Over."

"Sheriff, give me a day to get back to you," Goodwin said. "I'll have to make some calls. Over."

"No more than a day," Peck said. "I've got a situation here. Over."

"I'll see what I can do. Out."

Peck set the transmitter on the desk and looked at Kranston. "He'll see what he can do."

Kranston returned to Peck's desk, picked up his drink and finished it off in two large gulps. "I'm going home, Dave. I suggest you do the same and get some sleep. You won't be of any use to the state boys if you're a basket case."

"I'll stay here," Peck insisted. "I'm getting used to the cot."

"Suit yourself." Kranston walked to the door, and then paused as if he suddenly remembered something. "I almost forgot. Father Regan is preparing a memorial service for this Sunday. I thought it would be the appropriate time to make an announcement."

Peck stared at Kranston for several seconds. "Be prepared to answer the question why it took the second murder to announce the first."

Kranston gave a slight nod of his head to acknowledge he understood, turned and left the office.

Peck sat at his desk and wrote reports for several hours after Kranston left. Experience taught him that no detail was too small or insignificant to overlook or ignore. Most cases came to a successful conclusion by a second and third look at a detail detectives dismissed the first time. Once that missed detail became obvious, the detective usually beat himself up for not catching it sooner. Some day, police work would be a more advanced, highly technical science, but for now, it was keen eyes, instinct, experience and dedication. He hoped science and forensic labs didn't replace those invaluable qualities.

Peck fueled the fire, heated the coffee, and continued to write. Especially in murder cases, the twenty-four hour period before and after the crime was the most important. Once a scene grew cold, the less of a chance there was in solving the crime. In this instance, both murders were outside the window of solvability. Even the FBI crime lab would have a difficult time analyzing clues and finding a suspect.

Peck was reluctant to admit it, but that meant a third murder would have to occur in order to obtain enough fresh evidence to solve the first two. That was a homicide detective's nightmare, waiting out a fresh crime scene to solve a previous murder.

To the detective, a fresh crime scene meant new clues and a chance to close a case. To the victims, it meant they were dead.

It was as simple and as complicated as that.

Peck set his pen aside and gently rubbed a spot between his eyes just above his nose. He could not describe the feeling as pain, but pressure as if the area had suddenly swollen. As he sat there and rubbed, Peck's attention turned to the open door on the woodstove. Red-hot flames danced as the logs crackled. He could not explain why, but the flames appeared nearly hypnotic in their rhythm.

Peck placed both hands on the desk as he continued to stare at the fire. A bead of sweat rolled down his face to his mouth. It tasted of salt. He could feel his heart beating inside his chest and a vein swell on the side of his neck.

Suddenly, Peck was somewhere else, as if his mind was no longer connected to him and had left the room. It was impossible, he knew, but he felt as if his consciousness transported him to a place outside of his body and he was beside himself. He could see the flames of an out-of-control fire raging as if he were standing right before it. There were screams all around him, cries of pain ringing in his ears.

Peck jumped to his feet, but the hallucination stayed with him.

A tiny hand, a child's hand reached out for him.

Peck felt himself raise his right hand to reach for the child.

On contact with the child's hand, there was a sudden, thunderous explosion and the vision vanished like a puff of smoke. Drained, Peck fell backwards into his chair.

Sweat ran down his face as Peck tried to gather his thoughts and calm himself. He opened the desk drawer, removed the bottle of scotch and took a major-league swallow. Setting the bottle aside, Peck sat and stared at his fingers. He wanted to get up and return to the cot, but his legs felt like lead. He lit a cigarette and felt the muscles in his legs slowly relax. Finally, when he could stand without getting dizzy, he walked to the cot and drifted off to sleep almost instantaneously.

Peck joined McCoy for breakfast at Deb's Diner. News of Deb's death was unknown to her staff so the mood in the diner was cheerful, more so since the storm broke and the sky began to clear. Conversation was optimistic, almost festive. It was amazing how people came together in a time of emergency and could seemingly almost enjoy that emergency, then take pride that they survived it. Big-city and small-town people shared that quality across the country, Peck observed, remembering the nuclear bomb scares of the earlier fifties generation.

After they settled in at a table, Peck opened up to McCoy.

McCoy ate a spoon of oatmeal as he listened to Peck describe his nightmarish hallucination of the previous night. If McCoy was surprised at Peck's descriptive recounting, his face showed no emotion.

"I can't really describe it, Tom," Peck said. "It was as if I was having a dream and was wide awake at the same time."

"They did a study after the war," McCoy said.

"Which war, one or two?"

"Both, actually, but mostly from '46 to '49," McCoy said. "The study was on combat stress. They called it combat fatigue, mostly because it sounded better."

"I've been out of the Army thirteen years," Peck said.

"That doesn't matter. You were how old when you were drafted?"

"Thirty seven and I volunteered."

McCoy spooned some more oatmeal into his mouth and thought for a moment. "The war was hard enough on the young men, a guy your age at the time, it must have been hell."

"It was hell on everybody," Peck said. "But, I'm not getting this. If combat stress was behind this . . . hallucination, why now? The war has been over more than a decade."

"I'm not a shrink, Dave. I can only guess."

"Guess."

McCoy nodded. "Subjugation would be my first inclination."

"Come on, Tom, what the hell is that?"

"Long term repression."

"Repression? You think I've been sitting on this for a decade and a half?"

"It's possible," McCoy shrugged. "You came out of the war and went right back to work. In many ways, being a cop is like being a soldier. It is a high-stress job. There is no time or room for mistakes and certainly no time to reflect on the past. However, now you are retired and living in the middle of nowhere. All of a sudden, there are two very gruesome murders to contend with sandwiched between a crippling storm and the past catches up with you. Your mind starts to fatigue and you have post-traumatic, combat stress syndrome."

"Which is what exactly?" Peck said.

McCoy shrugged. "If I knew that, I'd be lecturing at the Surgeon General. Look, Army hospitals are full of men who suffered breakdowns from combat stress. They stare into space and see Germans under the bed and in the closets. They just don't know enough at this time to fix these poor bastards."

"Three times, I've dreamed of or hallucinated about fire," Peck said. "That has nothing to do with my combat experience, so I'm not making the connection."

"You aren't, but your subconscious mind is," McCoy said. "The man who dreams about falling or flying is actually dreaming about freedom, that kind of thing."

"What does fire represent?"

McCoy shrugged his shoulders. "That I don't know. I am not a psychiatrist. I will give the information to a doctor I know at Maine Med when I talk to him. I'm sure when all is said and done that you're fine."

Bender entered the diner and spotted Peck and McCoy and approached their table.

"There's a state police cruiser pulling up," Bender said.

Peck stood up from the booth. "About time."

Peck and Bender approached the state police car just as a tall, ramrod straight man of about fifty exited and stood on the curb. The man wore a dark suit and overcoat. He had the look of military about him, like a retired officer.

"I'm Sheriff David Peck, this is my deputy Jay Bender," Peck said.

"Lieutenant William Reese."

Reese and Peck shook hands and Peck noted that Reese had a solid and firm grip.

"Sorry about the delay, this storm," Reese said. "You have a place where we can talk?"

"The office," Peck said.

Peck and Bender took Reese to their office where a fire crackled in the woodstove and fresh coffee rested in a pot on top of it. Reese tossed his coat on a coat hook and looked around. "Cozy," he said.

"Coffee, Lieutenant?" Bender said, handing Reese a mug.

Reese sipped coffee from the chair opposite Peck's desk. "It's most unusual to have a double homicide in . . ."

"Not a double homicide," Peck corrected Reese. "Two homicides committed days apart in all likelihood by the same man."

Reese nodded. "Who are the victims?"

"Two white females in their mid- to late-forties."

"Is there any relationship between the two?"

Peck shrugged. "They both live in this town."

"And they're both dead," Bender added.

Peck and Reese looked at Bender. "I saw in an episode of *Perry Mason* once, the only clue they had to go one was that all the victims were dead. I forget how it ended."

"That may not be as far-fetched as you think," Reese said. "And I think I saw that episode."

Peck lit a cigarette, looking at Reese. "Other than both victims are dead, I have no leads, no clues and no suspects at this point. I have one murder weapon, which is a bread knife from the kitchen of the first victim. The second knife was probably tossed in the woods and won't be found until spring, if at all. This is a town in the middle of nowhere and cut off from the rest of the state until the roads are cleared, power is restored and phones are back on line. Where would you like to start?"

"Show me the victims?" Reese said. "That's usually a good place."

Peck and McCoy stood in the background while Reese inspected the body of Doris White, who was prone on a slab in the tiny hospital morgue. Wearing rubber gloves, Reese inspected the stab wounds, red marks on her neck and rope burns on the wrists. He took his time and when he touched the body, he was gentle, as if touching a baby.

"Had rigor set in when you found the body?" Reese said.

"Yes, by about twelve hours," McCoy said.

"The broken bones in the arms, legs and rib cage, they were caused by the tree?"

McCoy nodded. "She was dead a good eight hours before the tree came down."

"The second victim," Reese said.

McCoy moved forward to close the slab containing Doris White and pull out the one with Deb Robertson.

Reese moved up and down the body of Deb Robertson, touching her neck and wrists. "You check for rape?"

"Yes," McCoy said.

Peck turned away as Reese opened Deb's legs for a closer examination. "And what did you find?"

"There are definite signs of forced entry," McCoy said. "Irritation and swelling of the vaginal walls and membrane. Some minor bleeding."

"Rigor?"

"Not when the body was found."

"Time of death?"

"Between eleven and eleven-thirty."

Reese looked at Peck. "What time did you discover the body?"

"About twelve-twenty," Peck said.

"You just missed him then."

"Yes."

"Too bad," Reese said, shaking his head. "It would have made things easy."

"Yes."

Reese removed his gloves and tossed them into a trash can. "Is there a place we can talk?"

Reese sat at the table in the hospital lounge and sipped coffee as he looked at Peck.

Peck and McCoy sat at the table opposite Reese.

Reese said, "What are your thoughts, Sheriff?"

Peck lit a cigarette and took a sip of coffee before answering. "He's fueled by rage and very powerful. The markings on the necks of both women are deep and the stab wounds go clear to the handle of the knife. He even cut bone, not easy to do."

Reese nodded. "Anything else?"

"Tying the women to the bed was for pleasure, not necessity. He is easily strong enough to overpower both women if his goal was just rape and murder. There's something else going on."

McCoy stared at Peck, as did Reese. "You've worked homicide before?" Reese said.

"Baltimore. What's your take?"

Reese took a sip of coffee and said, "Without the benefit of seeing the crime scenes, I would guess that both women were selected at random by a man who didn't care who they were or what they looked like. To him they were just there."

"I'm just a country doctor," McCoy said. "So I'm a bit lost and a lot curious as to how you derived that."

Reese looked at Peck. "Care to enlighten the doctor, Sheriff?"

"One woman was beautiful, one was not," Peck said. "Looks didn't matter to him, only results."

McCoy thought for a moment. "The results being the rape or the murder?"

"Probably neither," Peck said. "In most cases like these, the killer has some inadequate feelings that need satisfying and uses his crimes to fulfill them."

"Like Mommy didn't give him enough attention?" McCoy said. "That kind of thing?"

"Possibly. Nobody knows for sure except the killer himself."

Reese looked at Peck. "We still have some daylight, Sheriff, feel like taking a ride?"

Four

Reese and Peck stood outside the trailer home of Doris White. Reese circled her old pickup, inspecting it, and then walked completely around the house with Peck following him. Reese carried a flip-open notebook and he used a pencil to make notations. They stopped at the remains of the front door where Reese quickly scanned the debris and rubble.

"No noticeable tire marks or footprints?" Reese said. "The snow and ice around the house are pretty much undisturbed except for the tree. You didn't see anything previously?"

"No, but whatever footprints or evidence might be here is under three inches of ice."

"Well, we can't exactly wait for spring." Reese entered the trailer, followed by Peck.

"We'll be fortunate to get anything from this mess, but I'll mark it for the forensic team," Reese said. He entered the bedroom, followed by Peck. "It's almost impossible to determine if there was a struggle."

"I don't think so," Peck said.

"Reason."

"Her pajamas. There wasn't a mark on them. Not a thread out of place. It was as if she removed them willingly."

"Which she may have under threat of harm," Reese said. "You've tagged them for evidence?"

"Yes."

Reese moved to the bedroom window and peered out through

the broken glass.

Peck looked at his watch. "There's enough daylight if you want to see the second site."

Reese nodded and they stepped outside the trailer.

Reese scraped ice off the windows of Deb Robertson's truck with a pocketknife and looked through the window at the keys, which still dangled in the ignition. "The engine was running when you arrived, you said?" Reese said, noting the ignition key was still in the start position.

"Stalled, but on," Peck said.

"Did she start the truck herself?"

"I don't know. Why?"

Reese turned to look at the house. "For a couple of reasons. She came down herself and the killer was hiding say in the woods nearby. He could have slipped into the house unseen. She would have walked into a trap. The other thing is if someone started the truck for her that someone could be our man. In any event, the truck and keys will be dusted for prints."

Reese removed a rubber glove from a pocket, covered the door handle, then opened the door and confiscated the keys using the glove. Locking the door, he closed it.

Peck started walking toward the house and Reese followed. "But you already thought of all that, didn't you?" Reese said.

"It occurred to me," Peck said.

They climbed the stairs and Peck used a key to unlock the door.

"What else has occurred to you?" Reese said as they stepped inside.

Peck drew his flashlight and clicked it on. Even in daylight, the house was dark and cold. "You tell me," Peck said.

They walked the house, room to room. Reese made notes along the way in his small notebook, using a pencil, which he continuously moistened with his tongue. Peck stayed in the background and did his best to remove his personal feelings and keep them from interfering with his instincts as a detective.

In the master bedroom, Reese paused and turned to Peck. "The killer wasn't a stranger. She let him in and went to the bedroom for something. That's when he surprised her. Maybe from behind. My team will be able to determine if she was choked into unconsciousness. At any rate, all the action took place in here."

"Because the downstairs is undisturbed," Peck said. "All the mess is up here."

Reese nodded as he jotted a note on his pad.

Peck said, "The thing of it is, in a town this small who is a stranger? Even if you don't know somebody's name, you're sure to recognize a face. Moreover, Deb ran the only diner. She must have seen and known just about everybody in town and half the paper mill. If someone were to come to her door for help, she would almost certainly let them in."

Reese snapped his pad shut and tucked it into a pocket. "My men will do a complete sweep of the house interior, exterior and her truck. Prints, hair, blood typing, the works. We might get lucky and find a set of prints that have no business being here."

"Have you seen enough?" Peck asked.

"For the moment, yes. Why?"

"I thought you might like to catch dinner before it's all gone."

"This turkey is delicious," Reese said as he ate a mouthful of the bird.

"That's because it's fresh."

Reese looked at Peck over his fork. "How fresh is fresh?"

"I think my deputy shot it this morning."

Reese smiled at Peck. "In times of extreme stress, nature will provide. My father always said that. However, when you said catch dinner, I didn't know you meant literally."

"Your father was a hunter?"

"A poacher," Reese said. "His life was nothing but one long train ride of extreme stress. He was arrested at least twenty times that I know of. He poached everything and anything he could shoot, but we were always well fed."

Peck looked around the diner. It was only half-full. Either people ate earlier or they were returning to their homes.

Reese ate another slice of turkey. "Do you have phones?"

"Not yet."

"Without power, this is going to be tough," Reese confessed. "We could run a generator, but we'll need a place to headquarter."

"There's an old logging camp just outside of town. It has a dozen cabins and a main hall where you could hook a generator. I've been there and it's pretty comfortable."

"Good."

"I'll show you where it is in the morning."

"About the victims, what can you tell me personally?"

"About Doris White, nothing. I never met the woman. Deb Robertson, more."

"How much more?"

Peck picked up his coffee cup and took a sip.

Reese nodded. "You were lovers."

"Briefly," Peck confessed. "It was in the beginner's stage, but if she lived, we might have had something. Funny, it was this damn storm which brought us together, and this damn storm which broke us apart."

"I'm sorry," Reese said. Then added, "Were you the last one to see her alive?"

"She came to work. Half the town saw her the day before she died. I'm in the half that didn't."

"My men will narrow down the list."

"What about Doris White?"

"We have to go with the freshest site. Find the killer of one, find the killer of both," Reese said.

The waitress who came to the office stopped by the table to freshen Peck's coffee. Peck stared at her.

"The other day when you asked me to check on Deb," Peck said. "You said Paco went to check on her. Do you know if he did?"

"I haven't seen him," the waitress said. "He won't be in until midnight to clean up and wash dishes."

"Thanks," Peck said.

The waitress freshened Reese's cup, nodded to Peck then returned to the counter.

Reese looked at Peck. "Who's Paco?"

"The dishwasher," Peck said. He looked at his watch. "It's only eight o'clock, feel like talking a ride?"

"To see this Paco?"

"Yes."

"Know where he lives?"

"I can find out."

"Let's go."

Peck drove his heavy cruiser along a back road on the northwest side of town. The moon was visible for the first time in a week. It was full and bright and its light reflected off the ice and snow, illuminating the ground well enough to see without a flashlight.

Peck turned off the dirt road and onto a fire road.

"This Paco . . . what's his last name?" Reese said.

"Ramirez."

"Right. What do we know about him?"

"His name. He washes dishes."

Reese turned his head to look at Peck. "This Paco might be

the last person to see the Robertson woman alive. We should find out a little more about him than his name."

"I thought that's what we were doing," Peck said.

Reese shook his head and allowed himself a tiny smile.

"Should be about another quarter mile," Peck said.

Ten minutes later, Peck rolled the cruiser to a stop twenty feet from the small mobile home where Paco Ramirez lived. Peck and Reese left the cruiser and walked to the front door, passing an old Ford pickup parked out front.

"He's home," Reese said, looking at the truck. "Looks like a '41 Ford."

Peck knocked on the front door of the trailer. "Paco Ramirez, this is Sheriff David Peck and Lieutenant Reese of the state police. We'd like a few words with you."

There was no response from inside the mobile home and after thirty seconds, Peck knocked again. "Paco, I know you're home. Your truck is here. Open up, please."

From around back there was the sound of a window opening and footsteps stomping on the ice.

"He's running," Reese said.

Peck dashed around to the rear of the mobile home just in time to see Paco run into the woods.

"Shit," Peck said and gave immediate chase.

As Paco ran, he attempted to slip into a winter jacket. After several attempts, he gave up and discarded it.

Peck slipped briefly on a patch of ice and Paco opened up a hundred-foot lead on him. In the distance, Peck could hear Reese's footsteps on the ice behind him.

Paco Ramirez was thin and built for speed like a sprinter. As he dodged trees in the woods, his lead opened to one hundred and twenty feet.

However, Peck was in excellent condition and ran like an athlete and left Reese far behind. The full moon helped keep

Paco in sight and Peck poured it on.

As Paco jumped a fallen tree, he began to tire. His thin body lacked the endurance of a distance runner. He glanced behind him and Peck had closed the distance to eighty feet. Paco sucked wind and sprinted harder, gasping loudly.

Peck pumped his arms and legs, took in air through his nose, and blew out through the mouth as if he were on an Army run of so long ago. He saw the gap closing, ignored the burning in his side, and pumped his arms harder. Slowly, the distance between the two men began to close.

When the gap was less than fifty feet, Paco ran completely out of steam, became confused from lack of oxygen, lost his bearings and began to run in circles.

Peck could hardly believe it when Paco turned around one hundred and eighty degrees and ran straight at him. At the last minute, Paco saw his mistake and attempted to do another one-eighty in midstep, but Peck was on him in an instant.

Peck tripped Paco with his leg and he landed hard and skidded ten feet across the ice. Peck pounced on him, twisting his arms behind his back.

Paco gasped for air. "Why you chase me?" he said in a thick Mexican accent.

"Why did you run?" Peck said.

"I run 'cause you chase me."

Peck snapped the cuffs on Paco's thin wrists and yanked him to his feet. "We'll walk back if that's okay with you, Paco?" Peck said. "And even if it isn't."

As Peck and Paco walked at a much slower pace back to the trailer, Reese emerged from the woods, gasping for air. Reese looked at Paco.

"You . . . have the . . . oh fuck, I can't breath," Reese gasped. "The right to . . . remain silent."

Reese paused, placed his hands on his knees and vomited on

Paco's shoes.

Paco turned and looked at Peck. "I juss buy those," Paco said.

Reese sucked wind and looked up at Paco.

Paco looked at his shoes. "What you have for dinner, turkey?"

In the cramped but tidy kitchen of Paco's trailer home, Paco served Peck and Reese thick, exceptionally strong Mexican coffee. A small generator hummed in the background and provided just enough power to run the lights and heater.

Sipping coffee, Reese lit a cigarette and looked at Paco. "Why did you run?"

"In Mexico, you don' run from the police you go to jail for things you don' do," Paco explained.

"This isn't Mexico," Reese said.

Paco set the coffee pot aside, sat at the round table opposite Peck, and slumped into his chair. "I thought you was the immigration about my green card."

"Green card?" Reese said. "What the hell are you talking about, green card? Paco, your boss is dead. Murdered. Who gives a fuck about your green card?"

Paco sat in stunned silence. He turned to look at Peck.

"Deb Robertson was murdered last night, Paco," Peck said. "Lieutenant Reese is a homicide investigator."

"That no can be," Paco finally said.

"It can be and it is," Reese said.

"But I juss see her juss yesterday," Paco said.

"Tell us about that," Reese said.

"The girls, they say to check on Miss Deb because she no come to work," Paco said. "I leave early and come to her house."

"You saw her?" Reese said.

"Yes."

"What time?"

"I leave at ten, maybe close to eleven by the time I get to Miss Deb's house."

"And she was okay?" Reese said.

"Yes, she fine."

"Did she come outside?" Peck asked.

"Yes, on the porch."

"What was she wearing?"

"Wearing?" Paco said. He shook his head. "I no remember."

Reese said, "Pants, a sweater, a jacket and hat? Or was she dressed for bed?"

"No, wait. She wear pants and a . . . how you say, a sweatshirt," Paco said. "And boots. She have on big, white boots."

"White boots?" Reese said.

Peck looked at Reese. "She had white snowmobile boots. She wore them the day I picked her up on my snowmobile."

"Yes, snowmobile boots," Paco said. "That's what they was."

"Paco," Peck said. "Can you remember anything of what she said? This is important."

"Yes. She say she could no sleep, that she wanted to take a ride maybe to town and check on her girls."

"And you started it for her?" Reese said.

Paco nodded. "She ask me to warm up her truck. She toss me down the keys."

"Then what did you do?" Reese said.

"I start the truck, scrape off the ice and then I go home."

Peck and Reese exchanged glances. Reese said, "Did you see anybody?"

"No."

"Did she talk to anybody, maybe somebody inside the house?" Reese said.

"No."

"You left her truck running?" Reese said.

"Yes, like she ask me to," Paco said.

"Were there any other cars parked alongside hers?" Peck said.

"No, no cars. Juss Miss Deb's truck."

Peck lit a cigarette as he mulled things over in his mind.

"Wait," Paco said. "There was a noise. I heard it from the woods."

"A noise?" Reese said. "What kind of noise?"

"A snowmobile," Paco said. "Somebody, they was riding a snowmobile."

"Were they close or far?" Peck said.

Paco shrugged. "I can no tell."

"But you're sure it was a snowmobile?"

"Yes."

Reese looked at Peck. "I didn't see any tracks."

"There aren't any."

"I know what I hear," Paco insisted. "Maybe it no come close to Miss Deb's house, but it was a snowmobile."

"Sound travels, especially at night," Peck said. "That snowmobile could have been a mile away and you would have heard it."

Paco leaned in across the table to look at Peck. "I come here three years ago to pick fruit," he said. "No one give me a job for the winter except Miss Deb. She teach me English, to read. Soon, I become citizen." A tear welled up in his right eye and he wiped it away. "You find who kill her. You find the man and you hurt him."

Reese looked at Peck.

"You make him pay," Paco said.

Reese and Peck stood up and left Paco alone. Just before the door closed, they heard him say, "You make him pay."

Peck closed the door from the outside and paused for a moment to listen to the sound of Paco crying. Peck looked at Reese, who shook his head. Together, they walked to the waiting cruiser.

Riding back to town in Peck's cruiser, Reese said, "Our man could have been scouting the house by snowmobile. Paco arrives in his truck and our man heads for the woods, returning after the coast is clear."

"Which brings us back to the killer wasn't a stranger theory," Peck said. "If Deb let him in of her own accord. He waits for Paco to leave and knocks on the door. Deb answers and sees a friendly, familiar face and lets the guy in. Maybe he told her he ran out of gas, whatever. The point is he got in without using force. That means we're not looking for a stranger."

"Right." Reese fell silent for a moment, and then said, "In a town this small, that is at least something."

Peck looked at Reese. "Yeah, what?"

Peck parked the cruiser in front of the municipal building. He and Reese exited and stood on the curb. Reese checked his watch.

"You wouldn't have anything in the way of a nightcap, would you, Sheriff?" Reese asked.

Peck added a log to the woodstove in his office, and then sat behind his desk.

Reese warmed his hands over the fire, rubbing them together, and then took the chair opposite Peck's desk. Peck opened a drawer and removed the bottle of scotch. "One finger or two?"

"Two," Reese said.

Peck poured scotch into plastic cups and set one on the desktop for Reese. "Sorry, no ice."

"These things take time," Reese said, picking up his cup. "A murder investigation can grow cold, be forgotten and then resurface and be solved six months later."

"After he kills again, is what you're saying," Peck said.

Reese took a gulp of scotch and nodded his agreement. "Let me ask you something, Sheriff? If you don't mind."

Peck lit a cigarette, took a sip of scotch. "Ask."

"What's the worst case you ever worked?" Reese said. "The absolute worst horror show, nightmare of your career."

Peck searched his memory for the one standout. "A two-year-old baby girl was found in a garbage Dumpster. She was raped and sodomized before the sick bastard suffocated her with a plastic bag and stuffed her body in a cat carrier."

Reese was speechless as he sipped from his plastic cup. Finally, he said, "Was she colored, the little girl?"

"She was."

"Did you ever catch the man responsible?"

"The boyfriend of the mother," Peck said. "He didn't want the responsibility of paying for the child. Sadly, neither did she. They planned the murder together, even taking the time to find a Dumpster, which wasn't emptied very often. They reported the baby kidnapped, but I suspected them right away because twenty years ago, who kidnaps a black baby in a poor neighborhood? It didn't add up so I took a closer look at the parents. The mother confessed first, saying she went along with the rape as a cover-up because the boyfriend said they would have a better life without the baby. The rest just fell into place."

"My worst, or at least the one which stands out in my mind," Reese said, "was in '55. A farm worker employed by the owner of a potato farm in Aroostook County didn't get the raise he wanted after a poor crop season. He took an ax to the farmer, his wife and two kids, the dog and cat and buried them all in the barn."

"You caught him?"

"No. He made it to New Hampshire where he hung himself in a five-dollar-a-night motel room. He left a suicide note explaining what he did and why. We excavated the barn for the remains. What a mess."

Peck finished his drink and poured another ounce into his cup. He held the bottle to Reese and topped off his as well.

"Our man," Peck said. "Is it the sex or violence which gets it done for him?"

"Hard to say," Reese admitted. "The FBI, the shrinks all say rape is a crime of violence. I would guess they would say the murder is to mask the rape."

"But you don't agree?"

"I'm a cop, not a psychiatrist," Reese said.

"What kind of crime is murder?" Peck said.

"If you're talking about our man, I would say it's both."

"He likes the sex and he enjoys the violence," Peck said. "A double whammy."

"How I see it."

"That means he won't stop."

"No," Reese said. "He won't."

Peck took a final sip of his drink. Reese did the same and stood up. "Is there room at the inn across the street?"

"If you mean the hospital, half the people have returned home."

"I'll see you for breakfast," Reese said.

"I hope you like oatmeal," Peck said.

Reese paused at the door to turn around. "Sheriff, that vomiting episode back there, that's between us."

Peck nodded his head. "Goodnight, Lieutenant."

Five

An hour after Reese left his office; Peck was still wide-awake. He knew he was running on adrenaline. He knew that he was physically and mentally exhausted, but he also knew sleep would be next to impossible in his present state of mind. He added several logs to the woodstove, lit a cigarette and looked out the window.

The full moon cast an eerie, yellowish glow on Main Street. A lone candle burned in a window of the hospital. The church and diner were dark and gloomy.

A cloud passed in front of the moon and it glowed brightly in a band of silver and gray streaks. Peck lit another cigarette, knowing he needed to sleep, but he was unable to tear himself away from the moon's attraction.

Somewhere, far in the distance, a coyote howled.

From the bedroom in his private quarters in the hospital, McCoy opened his eyes when the light of the moon shown so brightly through the window it struck him across the face and woke him up.

McCoy got out of bed, slipped on his robe, and went to the window. The gigantic moon hung low in the sky, brightly illuminating the sky in a mixture of dark blue against twinkling stars. Clouds appeared white and silver to the eye. McCoy could see the outline of pine trees in the distance. He looked at his watch. It was nearly two in the morning. He knew he should return to bed, that he had a great deal to do in the morning, but he was so captivated by the moon he couldn't tear himself away from the window.

Finally, out of desperation, McCoy forced himself to return to bed. He slipped under the covers and lay perfectly still to wait for sleep to overtake him. Instead, he was more wide-awake than ever.

Far away, traveling on the night winds, he heard a coyote howl.

Regan was unable to sleep. Although he was certainly tired enough, the vision of Doris White and Deb Robertson weighed heavily on his mind. The priest dressed in a robe, crossed the hallway from his small apartment to the private chapel reserved for baptismal and other ceremonies. He knelt at the small altar and prayed for strength, guidance and wisdom.

As he prayed, Regan suddenly noticed the bright moonlight filtering in through the stained-glass chapel window. The sight of the brilliantly colored glass image of our Lord, Jesus Christ was hypnotic. He stood and went to the window, opened it and gasped. The sight was spellbinding as the moon passed before a group of clouds and brought a smile to his lips. God was awake and looking down upon the Earth, blessing it with his beauty.

Somewhere, off in the distance, a coyote howled.

Linda Boyce celebrated her thirtieth birthday a few weeks earlier by spending one hundred and ten dollars on a new winter comforter. It was a pale white with a star pattern and thick with down, guaranteed to keep you warm on the coldest nights.

By candlelight, she brushed her hair in front of the bedroom dresser mirror. She may have been thirty, but she didn't look it, so everybody said. She took exceptional care of her skin, used creams and moisturizers and avoided the sun during the summer months. During winter, with the dry heat, she took extra precautions, using lotion and cold cream twice a day. At five foot four, she weighed the one-eighteen of her high school graduation.

She put the brush down and inspected her shoulder-length black hair. She was proud of the fact she lacked a single strand of gray. Her green eyes were flawless, the skin around them unlined or blemished. Only her breasts betrayed her age, that she was no longer a girl of twenty-one. While still firm, they had gentle sag and a hint of stretch marks that were imperceptible to a stranger, but stood out like a beacon to her. Still, by anyone's standards she was a knockout.

It was no wonder she could command twenty-five dollars a trick. Even more if she operated in a big town like Augusta or Portland. She had thought about it, moving to a city, but always put it off. For one thing, the bigger the city the greater the risks. For another, the chances of facing arrest for solicitation out here in the sticks were slim to none. Besides, she was saving her money and when she had enough, there would be other career considerations. For now, she was content with her modest status in life.

Linda left the bedroom of her tiny mobile home and went to the kitchen for a beer. She had not run the generator in two hours, but the bottle was still cold. Even the ice trays were still semi-frozen.

She lit a cigarette and checked the battery-run clock on the wall over the refrigerator. She had time to finish the beer and maybe have another cigarette.

She carried the beer to the bedroom where she removed all of her clothes and slipped on a sheer, black nightgown. Goose bumps rose up on her arms. She brushed her teeth and used a mouthwash because men hated the smell of cigarettes on a woman's breath. Then she flipped down the comforter and crawled into bed to warm herself and to wait and maybe have a nap.

At two a.m., she heard Harvey Peterson arrive in his truck. She heard the engine shut off and the truck door open. She heard him walk to her front door, open it and enter her trailer.

"Linda?" Harvey called to her.

"The bedroom," she replied. "And it's about time."

Harvey entered the bedroom and smiled at her when he saw her tucked in like that. Kittenish was the word that came to mind.

"I waited up for you," Linda said.

Harvey tossed his jacket and immediately removed his shirt. He was a good-looking man, tall and well built, a cheerleader's dream.

"How much to stay the night?" Harvey said. "I'm too tired for the drive home."

He sounded Canadian, but it was difficult to tell. She hadn't been home to her small town north of Sherbrook, Quebec, for so long she had lost the ear for the dialect.

"I wouldn't throw you out, Harv," Linda said. "Not on a cold night like this. Twenty-five and we'll call it even."

Harvey grinned at her as he dropped his pants. He was already excited.

"Only hurry up. I'm freezing."

Harvey slid into bed next to Linda and reached for her. She winced at his touch.

"Your hands are like ice," Linda complained.

"You'll just have to warm me up then," Harvey said.

Linda crawled on top of him and Harvey closed his eyes. Neither of them paid any attention to the tiny bedroom window in the corner of the room, or the bright moonlight, which filtered in. Had either of them taken the time to notice, they would have been shocked to see the ski-masked figure of a man watching them through the window.

He wore a dark jacket with matching pants and boots. The gloves on his hands were also black, as was the ski mask. Only his eyes were visible and in the moonlight, they appeared a peculiar shade of yellow. As he watched Harvey and Linda make love, he could hear her soft moans and cries of pleasure, his disgusting, animalistic grunts. Anger rose up in his stomach. His hands balled into tight fists and shook violently as his anger became uncontrolled rage.

Turning away from the window, he ran into the woods and vanished into the dark cover of night.

Staring out the window, Peck had forgotten about the lit cigarette until it burned his fingers. He dropped it to the floor and stepped on it with his boot. Stupid, he told himself.

The coyote continued to howl.

Turning away from the window, he tossed several logs into the woodstove and stirred things up until the fire was roaring again. He stripped to his underwear and tossed a blanket on the cot. Before extinguishing the candles, he removed Doctor McCoy's pills from his desk and set them aside where they would be handy.

He looked at his watch as he settled in on the cot. It was just after two a.m. As if saying goodnight, the coyote howled several times in succession. Peck closed his eyes with the coyote's haunting cry echoing in his ears.

Six

Peck was up at seven, made a fire, and then ran the generator long enough for the water to heat. In the hallway bathroom, he shaved and washed his face and used a splash of Aqua Velva to take the sting off. Back in his office, he dressed in a twice-worn uniform and met Reese for breakfast by eight.

The diner was crowded, but not full. Peck and Reese shared a table by the window. As he sipped coffee, Peck noted that there was actually street and pedestrian traffic on Main Street. If people were able to venture out on foot and in vehicles, he took that as a sign things were beginning to return to normal.

Reese spooned oatmeal into his mouth. "God awful stuff," he commented. "I'll radio my men to stock up on supplies before they leave. A week of this oatmeal and I'll not only go nuts, I'll permanently lose my appetite."

"You can use my shortwave to call your men," Peck said.

Reese ate another spoon of oatmeal and washed it down with coffee. "My men could be here as early as five this afternoon if I can get through to them. In the meantime, I suggest we begin interviews. We might get lucky and find somebody who's a bit too nervous or maybe noticed a stranger or drifter."

"This is a small town, Lieutenant. Even by Maine standards, it's a small town."

"Meaning?"

"A stranger, a drifter is going to stick out like a sixth finger."

"You think he's keeping to himself or gone underground?"

"Or is hiding right out in the open for all to see."

Reese took a sip of coffee and looked at Peck. "That is possible, but unlikely. I feel our best bet is to target the unknown."

"That unknown has forty-seven square miles to hide in," Peck said. "It would take six months to find him given our limited resources, if our man proves to be a stranger."

"I'll go out on a limb and guess that you're leading up to something."

Peck sipped coffee, set aside his cup and lit a cigarette. "The governor has the authority to activate the National Guard in a crisis. We have two murders wedged between the ice storm of the century. I'd say that qualifies."

Reese nodded his agreement. "I'm sure the governor has the Guard already mobilized and committed elsewhere, but I'll put through your request to his office when I speak to my men. Until we get an answer, I suggest we make the most with what we have available."

Linda Boyce enjoyed watching men eat. They were not like women in that regard. They wolfed their food down, ate with gusto and embellished each bite as if it were their last. They weren't afraid to burp, either. Women were like birds, picking away at their meal as if afraid to be seen enjoying their food. She knew she was guilty of just such behavior, taught to her by her mother at a young age. When alone, she ate like a starving wolf cub, but in the company of a man, it was a habit she just couldn't seem to shake.

"Men don't want to see a woman eat like a pig," her mother would say at the dinner table when she was a young girl.

What Mother never knew, or chose to ignore, was that men did not care how a woman ate just so long as she delivered in the bedroom. Linda found that out when she was sixteen and the men came home from the war, desperate for female companionship and more than willing to part with some of their war treasure in exchange for some of her feminine treasure. It proved to be a profitable exchange.

Harvey was up with the sun and insisted he was starving. He said he had a full day's work ahead of him at the paper company and she took the hint. She made a fire in the small woodstove, then ran the generator long enough to scramble eggs and fry some bacon. She made coffee, which was all she took in the morning, along with a cigarette.

Harvey spooned eggs into his mouth and washed it down with coffee. "I'm off at midnight. I'd like to stop by again."

Linda took a sip of coffee as she looked at him. "How can you afford that, sugar? I know what the paper mill pays."

Harvey grinned at her. "I got a nice Christmas bonus and I can't think of a better way to spend it."

"Okay, but listen. I have to charge you for overnight. That's forty dollars and bring some groceries, the way you eat."

"Some steaks, how's that?" Harvey said. "A nice bottle of liquor."

"In that case, bring a bottle of scotch. Chivas."

Harvey nodded and stood up. "I will, but right now I gotta go."

Reese got through to Augusta on Peck's shortwave radio without much of a problem. He spoke to several of his men, put through a food list and relayed Peck's request for the National Guard. After signing off, Reese told Peck that maybe things were not back to normal yet, but there was progress.

Peck sipped coffee from his desk and watched Reese. Ed Kranston walked into the office just as Reese signed off and returned the headset to its stand.

"Good morning," Kranston said, chewing his customary gum. "Any news from the radio?"

"The good news is I reached the emergency center in Augusta," Reese said. "My men will be here as soon as possible and with additional food supplies. I'm also told phone lines will be up and running within a week. Two weeks for power to return statewide."

Kranston reached for the coffeepot on the woodstove and poured a cup. He turned and looked at Reese. "What's the bad news?"

"A nor'easter is on the way," Reese said. "A foot of new snow is expected the day after tomorrow."

"For crying out loud," Kranston said. "We need to catch a break here."

Peck lit a cigarette and looked at Kranston. "I've invited the lieutenant and his men to use the old logging camp outside of town as a headquarters."

Kranston looked at Reese. "It's comfortable. I've been out there with the code enforcement officer when they redesigned some of the zoning laws. At least that's something."

Reese looked at Peck with a grin in his eye. "Yeah, what?"

"It's . . . well, I don't know," Kranston stammered.

Peck looked at Kranston, who appeared somewhat ill at ease.

"I'll be in my office," Kranston said. "I have some . . . you know."

Kranston reached the door, paused and looked at Peck. "Good luck today, Dave."

"With?"

"Whatever it is you and the lieutenant are doing."

Kranston left the office and Peck looked at Reese. "What are we doing?"

By five-thirty in the afternoon, Peck and Reese were back in Peck's office. Reese occupied Bender's desk, while Peck sat behind his own. A fire in the woodstove crackled in the background. A half dozen candles and the kerosene lantern burned for the necessary light they needed to read and write reports.

Sipping coffee, Reese looked up from his notes at Peck. "Would you care to sweeten this, Sheriff?"

Peck opened the desk drawer for the scotch bottle. It was nearly half-empty. Peck dumped an ounce into his coffee mug, and then crossed the room to pour another ounce into Reese's cup.

"How many people we talk to this afternoon?" Reese said, sampling his sweetened coffee.

"I've got a count of twenty-nine on my list. You?"

Reese scanned his sheets. "Thirty, at best."

Peck returned to his desk and lit a cigarette.

Reese took another sip from his mug. "How many would you say are innocent?"

"Innocent of what?"

Reese grinned at Peck. "At least the two murders."

"All of them. What about your list?"

Reese leaned back in his chair. "Some of them are guilty of something. Poaching chickens, maybe, but no murderers I could see."

"Yet."

Reese nodded and looked at the cigarette in Peck's hand. "Can you spare one, Sheriff?"

Peck tossed his pack across the room. Reese removed one and lit it from a candle. "Ever smoke Lucy's?"

Peck hadn't heard the term Lucy's in years. "Sure. When I was a kid, that's all I could afford." Before the war, you could walk into any tobacco store, grocery store or newsstand anywhere in the country and buy loose cigarettes for a penny apiece. "The gas station across the street still sells them that way. So does the drugstore."

"I used to fool myself into thinking I could quit by smoking Lucy's," Reese said. "Buy only five in the morning and stretch them out all day. By noon, I'd be bumming smokes from anyone who would give them to me."

"In the Army, they would issue a pack of four with K-rations," Peck said. "The cigarettes would be so stale, we'd toss them and buy Lucy's and reuse that pack for months."

The office door suddenly opened and Bender came in, stomping his feet. "Christ's sake, it's starting to snow."

"Looks like the nor'easter's decided to show up early," Reese said.

Bender looked at Reese. "Your men are here. Two vans and a cruiser pulled up outside."

Peck said, "Why don't you take the cruiser and run the lieutenant and his men to the logging camp, Jay. I think we're done here today and I'm sure he'd like to get settled in."

Reese folded his notes and stood up. "See you for breakfast, Sheriff?"

Peck nodded.

Bender said, "Come on, Lieutenant. Let's see if we can beat the storm and get you and your men tucked in for the night. You got plenty of firewood compliments of the paper company."

"That's very nice of them," Reese said. "I'll be sure they get a letter of thanks from the office."

After they left, Peck busied himself for several hours with reports and notes to himself. He ate a quick meal at the diner where he sat alone and read reports. Afterward, feeling exhausted, he decided to turn in early.

Peck awoke when a slight feeling of heaviness behind his sinuses forced him to open his eyes. He stood up from the cot, feeling slightly dizzy and congested and tossed a log into the woodstove, then went to his desk and lit a candle. Sitting, he opened the drawer for the bottle of pills given to him by Doctor McCoy. He swallowed one without water, and then sat back in the chair to wait for the medicine to take effect.

On the desk, the tiny flame of the candle cascaded its light over the desk, creating flickering shadows on the wall. Peck's eyes moved to the flame and focused on it. He could feel the medicine begin to kick in, relaxing the muscles in his face, easing the pressure behind his eyes, opening his sinuses.

The flame of the candle danced and flickered. Shadows whirled around the room in a waltz-like dance in syncopation with the tiny flame. Peck was all but mesmerized by flame and shadow. He had the urge to move, but found his hands were locked in place on the desk. McCoy's pills, whatever they were, packed a wallop. He could feel his eyelids grow heavy and the room became slightly out of focus.

Suddenly, a child's hand appeared to reach out of the candle flame and beckon to him. As the small hand reached for Peck, the flame of the candle appeared to grow and spread. It appeared to illuminate the entire office.

Peck blinked his eyes, knowing that he was experiencing some kind of side effect of the medication, but the flames only grew larger and more severe. Sweat began to roll down his face, but he was unable to move and wipe it away, so powerful was the tug of the candle and the effect of the drug.

From the center of the flames, the child's hand stretched toward Peck, reaching for him. Fascinated by his hallucination, he raised his hand toward the child's and just before contact, there was the loud cry of a child's pain.

Peck jumped up from his chair as his head all but exploded from pent-up pressure behind his eyes. He held onto his skull tightly, waiting for the pain to lessen, but it only increased. Blowing out the candle, Peck stumbled to the cot and fell on top of it. He closed his eyes and the pressure mounted to a new level. Nearly unable to cope, Peck held his head and wondered if he was having a stroke and tonight would be the night he would die.

Snow fell lightly as he walked in near total darkness through the woods. Shrouded by the ski mask, he appeared ominous, like a crazed madman as only the whites of his eyes were visible. At a clearing in the woods, he paused to stare at the mobile home of Linda Boyce. Then, slowly, he made his way toward it. As he neared the home, his hands clenched into fists with anticipation of what was to come.

Like a kid on Christmas morning, he thought.

At eleven p.m., Linda powered up the generator so she could take a hot bath before Harvey arrived from his shift at the paper mill. She busied herself by making a roaring fire in the woodstove and at eleven-thirty, she tested the water. It was ready and she filled the tub with her most expensive bubble bath. Harvey, despite his prodigious appetite for food and sex, liked the way her skin smelled and felt and took the time to compliment her on it.

Peck moaned to himself as the throbbing pressure and stabbing pain in his head appeared to worsen. Fearful that he would not last the night, he forced himself to stand up from the cot and stumbled through the dark on wobbly legs to his desk for the bottle of pills. As he twisted the cap off the bottle, a razor sharp pain hit him between the eyes and he fell to his knees. The bottle of pills jarred from his grasp and rolled away.

From the exterior of the bathroom window of her mobile home, he crouched in darkness and watched as the robe slowly fell away from Linda's body and she entered the tub of hot, soapy, scented bubble bath.

At the sight of her nude body, he felt his pulse quicken and a knot form in his chest. He was about to turn away from the window when she began to shave her legs with a razor. The procedure fascinated him and he watched, spellbound as she ran the razor up one creamy thigh and down another. He all but fainted when she turned her attention to her pubic hair and neatly cleaned up with gentle flicks of the razor. Breathing rapidly from his excitement, he felt lightheaded and giddy the way that children did on Christmas morning when they knew the present they wished and hoped for was actually under the tree waiting for them to unwrap it.

Forcing himself to turn away from the window, his eyes searched for a weapon and settled on a stack of firewood.

On the floor of his office, Peck crawled toward the bottle of pills, which rolled halfway across the floor towards Bender's desk. The effort caused the pain to worsen, but he finally reached the bottle only to discover the cap was missing and the pills were scattered on the floor.

Linda rinsed the razor clean, then tossed it into the sink. She reached for a bottle of baby oil on the floor and rubbed some onto her legs and around her pubic area to avoid razor burn. Satisfied with the results, Linda lowered herself into the hot, scented water and sipped from a glass of wine and felt all of her troubles melt away. Three candles burning on the sink gave the mood just the right amount of romantic atmosphere. She had tried the portable transistor radio, but all she could get was loud static, but she didn't really mind. The peace and quiet was reassuring in a way. She did not hear his truck, but the front door suddenly opened. Who else could it be but Harvey?

"Harvey? Sugar, is that you? Did you remember the scotch?"

Linda called out. "Chivas like I asked you to?"

Peck crawled around, feeling the floor for the pills until he finally located two. He swallowed them and then tucked himself into the fetal position on the floor to wait for them to take effect. He tried his best not to vomit or pass out.

Linda drank the last bit of wine in her glass and set it on the rim of the tub. She heard footsteps outside the bathroom door and called out to Harvey again.

"Harvey, I'm in the tub."

Without warning, the door smashed inward with a loud crash and the man in the ski mask suddenly appeared. A thick log from the firewood pile was in his right hand. Before she could move or react, he swung the club against the side of Linda's head. She felt an explosion inside her skull, then she felt nothing at all.

In the main hall of the logging camp, Reese's men entertained themselves with card games and rounds at the pool table. A fire crackled in the massive stone fireplace. Reese occupied himself with reading reports at the sofa, aided by a powerful kerosene lantern which rested on the coffee table directly in front of him.

Reese suddenly closed his report book and checked his watch. "It's getting late, gentlemen. I am going to bed. I suggest you do the same."

At the pool table, Harvey Peterson banked a shot to win his game. He tossed his pool stick on the table as Reese opened the front door of the cabin. Pausing, Reese said, "We'll breakfast at eight, then head to town. Last man out, make sure the generator is off and wood is stacked for the morning."

Harvey waited to make certain Reese was safely in his cabin, then snuck out the front door and walked to his truck. The other men in the squad did not question his actions. They all knew what an insatiable hound he was when it came to women. Besides, Harvey was reliable, never late and good at his job, so who cared if he spent his nights sniffing around.

Linda opened her eyes and her first thought was that she had gone blind from the blow to her head. She had never experienced such pure darkness before in her life. Slowly, as the fog inside her head lifted and consciousness became clear, she realized that her eyes and mouth were wrapped with duct tape.

She tried to move her arms and legs and felt the coarseness of rope binding her to the bed. She realized at that moment she was about to die.

There was a noise, a footstep, then she felt the tape pulled from her eyes, removing skin from her face and hair from her eyebrows. Her screams of pain and fear were lost inside the tape binding her mouth.

She waited, counted to thirty, waited some more and then opened her eyes.

Harvey opened the door to his truck as quietly as possible. He was about to step inside the cab when Reese came into the light from whatever shadow he had been hiding in and yanked on the door. It scared Harvey shitless.

"I won't tolerate lateness, sloppy work or a man too tired to perform his duties," Reese said.

"I . . . forgot something," Harvey said.

"What's the name of the little floozy you forgot?" Reese said.

Harvey grinned as he entered his truck. "Don't wait up, boss. You need your sleep, an old guy like you."

"Not so old I can't figure out what you're up to." Reese stuck his face in the door before Harvey closed it. "Just you remember what I said and that your ass is here for roll call."

"Count on it," Harvey said and started the engine. "Me and my ass."

Reese stared at Harvey as he put his truck in gear and drove away.

A lone candle flickered on the bedroom dresser. When she opened her eyes, it took a few seconds for them to grow accustomed to the dark and focus. She searched the room until she saw him sitting in a chair against the wall, watching her through a dark ski mask. By the dim light of the candle, his eyes appeared yellow and crazed. In a fit of panic, she struggled against the ropes. His eyes showed delight at her struggle, as if smiling at her. The tape on her mouth prevented her from screaming. After a few minutes, the rope began to burn her skin and she quieted down. She could see the disappointment in his eyes as she lay still.

The pain in his head was like an elephant sitting on his skull. Peck wondered if he had a blood clot or tumor, if McCoy overlooked something seriously wrong inside his head. He rolled onto his stomach and crawled along the floor to the gravity-fed water cooler. The effort made his head hurt even worse and his muscles ached and cramped. Reaching the cooler, he turned onto his back, flipped the switch and cold, clear water washed down and hit him in the face. It had a numbing effect and he let the water run for as long as he could stand it, then turned the water off. He shivered from cold, but at least the pain quelled a bit from the combination of pills and ice water.

Linda's eyes didn't move from the man in the ski mask. He sat in the chair for what seemed like an eternity. She couldn't tell if he was breathing, he was so motionless. His yellow eyes were locked onto her and when she wiggled her leg to ease an itch, she could see the whites of those yellow eyes follow her movement. What was funny, she knew she was minutes away from certain death at the hands of this madman, yet she thought about the taste of glue from the tape in her mouth. Sour and sticky, she choked back a gag, knowing that if she vomited she would die from suffocation. So instead, she would die with a tongue full of post office glue as the last thing she would ever taste.

Suddenly, his right hand slowly moved as he raised it to a spot just above his nose and gently rubbed as if he had a headache. She had seen her mother do that whenever she had a headache caused by the weight of her heavy framed glasses resting on the bridge of her nose. She wondered if he wore glasses like her mother.

After several minutes of massaging the spot between his eyes, the man in the ski mask raised himself from the chair and stood at the foot of the bed. His yellow eyes scanned her spread-eagle body. She could feel those yellow eyes searching and settling at the opening between her legs. With a gloved hand, he touched her foot and her entire body seemed to jerk on contact. The eyes inside the mask appeared to smile and take delight in the panic she displayed at his touch.

He moved the hand up her calf to her thigh and she fought with all of her strength against the ropes, and his eyes showed the pleasure he took in her helplessness. Fear overtook her and tears rolled down her cheeks. He paused to look at her face, and then reached out to touch a tear with a gloved hand and inspect it as if seeing a tear for the first time in his life. He wiped the tear on his shirt and stared into her eyes.

Determined not to give him any additional pleasure, Linda forced herself to remain calm. Maybe it would help defuse the situation if she showed him he hadn't gotten the better of her. Except that he had.

Long seconds passed before he spun around and returned to the chair where he reached down and picked up a large bread knife that she recognized as one of her own from a set in the kitchen. He turned, holding the knife in his left hand. With his right hand, he opened the belt to his pants and exposed his erection.

Inside the duct tape, unable to control her fear any longer, Linda screamed.

The clock in the dashboard of his truck read twelve-thirty when Harvey arrived at Linda's trailer home. On the front seat rested a bag of groceries and a bottle of Chivas Regal scotch, twenty-five years old. He knew that Linda would be pleased at the gift and hoped she would show her gratitude with a little extra care in the sack.

He parked the truck next to Linda's beat up old car and hopped out with the bag of groceries in his arms. He went directly to the unlocked front door, opened it and stepped inside.

"I'm here," Harvey shouted.

Linda wasn't sure what frightened her most, the sight of his fully erect penis or the bread knife in his left hand. Just then, with his pants down around his ankles she heard Harvey arrive in his truck. The man in the ski mask froze in his tracks as Harvey's truck engine went silent. She heard the front door open and Harvey called out to her. The man in the ski mask turned his head toward the bedroom door and his erection began to wilt as his sexual excitement turned to anger.

He yanked his pants up and looked at Linda with livid, hate-filled eyes as if the disruption were somehow her fault.

Holding the paper bag of groceries, Harvey went to the tiny kitchen and set the bag on the table. The room was dark and he took the time to light a candle, and then removed the bottle of scotch from the bag. "Linda, are you in the tub again? I got your scotch."

Harvey peeled off the wrapper from the cap and opened the bottle. "Linda?" he shouted. "Can you hear me? Where are you?"

Harvey grabbed two glasses from the counter top and carried them and the bottle to the bedroom. The door was open and the bedroom was so dark it was impossible to see anything.

"Linda?" Harvey said. "Are you in there?"

Harvey entered the bedroom, scanning the dark interior with his eyes. As his night vision improved, the faint outline of Linda became visible on the bed. "What the hell is . . . what are you doing?"

The man in the ski mask appeared from behind the door and shoved the bread knife into Harvey's stomach with such speed and force, Harvey was not aware that he had been stabbed until the Chivas bottle slipped from his grasp and fell to the floor.

The man in the ski mask brought his face nose to nose with Harvey and shoved the knife deeper into Harvey's flesh, grunting loudly at the effort. Then he released the knife handle, backed away and looked at Harvey with hate-filled eyes. And just like that, he was gone.

"What?" Harvey said, feeling his warm blood run down his stomach. He looked at the knife that protruded from a bloody wound just above his naval. Only the handle was visible. Faint light from the kitchen filtered in behind him and he looked at Linda on the bed. She twisted and fought with the ropes as she watched him slump to his knees.

"Oh God," Harvey gasped when the pain and realization kicked in.

Linda watched helplessly as Harvey took hold of the knife with both hands and slowly withdrew it from his stomach, crying and jerking as the blade inched its way from his flesh. He nearly passed out, the pain was so intense, but he forced himself to stay cognizant. Finally, the knife was free and as it fell to the floor, he looked at her. "Help me, please," he said. "Linda."

She struggled with all of her strength, but it was no use, the ropes held tight and she was helpless to do anything. Harvey bent to pick up the knife and fell to all fours and lay still for several seconds. Having no choice he slowly crawled toward the bed. It took him more than a minute to cover the distance of ten feet to the bed. To Linda, watching him inch along, crying out in pain and leaving a trail of blood behind him, it seemed like an hour. Finally, he reached her right arm and somehow found the strength and used the bloody knife to cut her free of the ropes. The knife fell from his grasp as she jumped off the bed and knelt to Harvey.

Jesus Christ, his blood was everywhere.

"My truck," Harvey said, weakly. "There's a radio. Use it to call for help."

Without warning, the pain in his head was gone. No lessening of pressure or slow reduction of pain, the way a headache fades away to nothing when properly medicated. It was suddenly and completely gone as if it never struck him to begin with.

Peck stood up on weak legs and steadied himself against the water cooler. His T-shirt and underwear were soaking wet with ice-cold water and a chill ran through his body. He stripped off shirt and shorts and stood before the woodstove. The heat from the fire quickly warmed him and returned some of the strength to his legs. He rubbed the muscles and stomped his feet to get circulation moving again.

Behind him, the shortwave radio on Bender's desk suddenly crackled to life. A female voice said, "Please help me. Is anybody out there? A man has been stabbed. Can anybody hear me? Please."

Naked, Peck ran to Bender's desk, nearly slipping in a puddle of water and grabbed the microphone. "This is Sheriff David Peck. I can hear you."

"Help. Help me, please," the voice of Linda Boyce cried.

Bender kept the cruiser overnight at his house so Peck took one of the snowmobiles, which enabled him to cut through the woods and make much better time along the unplowed, back roads to the residence of Linda Boyce. He had to check the map on the wall before he left and mark the fire road she lived on. Traveling at maximum speed, he made the trip in just under thirty minutes.

Peck arrived at the Boyce trailer where he parked the snowmobile next to a new pickup truck. Linda Boyce, completely naked, huddled with her arms wrapped tightly across her chest for warmth, sat in the front seat. Wide-eyed with fear and shivering, she looked at him.

"I'm Sheriff David Peck," Peck said, shining his flashlight into the truck. Blood was on her face and arms.

She shivered from cold and fear as she looked at Peck. "Don't make me go in there. Please. I don't want to go in there."

"What's in there?" Peck said.

She looked at him. "He's dead."

"Who is dead?"

"Harvey. He's dead. He killed him with a knife. Please don't make me go in there."

Peck removed his jacket and gave it to Linda and she wrapped it around her shoulders. Blood was on her face and arms. He spotted the keys in the ignition and said, "Start the truck and run the heat."

Linda turned the key, the truck fired to life, and she clicked the button on the dashboard for heat.

Peck drew his .357 Magnum revolver. "Stay here, stay calm and don't move until I return."

Peck turned away from the truck and slowly entered the small mobile home. He scanned the immediate area with his flashlight, and then moved to the bedroom. Although expecting the worst, he was still shocked at the horrific sight of the dead man on the floor by the nightstand.

Whoever he was, he left this world hard. A long trail of blood traced his path from the bedroom door to the nightstand where he died face down on the floor. The pool of blood under the body appeared black and thick, a sign that the knife had pierced his liver or a lung. Peck removed rubber gloves from a pocket, slipped them on and looked at the man's face. He was young, maybe all of thirty. He was also large and powerful, with enormous hands and thick shoulders. Peck figured he was taken by surprise so his strength was not a factor in the outcome.

Peck returned to the truck and opened the door. "You called me on a radio."

Linda pointed to the portable shortwave radio mounted under the dashboard. "He said I should call for help."

"Move over," Peck said and entered the truck.

By the time Reese and his army of men arrived, it was after two-thirty in the morning. The lack of sleep showed on Reese's face and in his tired, bloodshot eyes.

Earlier, Peck found a pair of jeans and a sweater for Linda Boyce and moved her inside to the kitchen. He built a fire in the small woodstove and ran the generator for heat, and still her teeth chattered, and she shook uncontrollably. They were sipping hot coffee when the small band of vehicles pulled up outside of Linda's mobile home.

The first thing Reese said when he walked into the tiny trailer was, "I recognize the truck. It belongs to my man Harvey Peterson."

Peck stood up from the tiny table and led Reese into the bedroom. "He's a cop, a state trooper?"

"A corporal with great potential. A good man if somewhat undisciplined." Reese nodded as he knelt down to the body and turned it over. "Oh Harvey, you dumb bastard." Reese sighed loudly.

"What was he doing here?" Peck said.

Reese stood up. "Good question. Maybe we should ask her?"

Linda was trying to sip coffee from a mug when Peck and Reese reentered the kitchen. Her hand shook so violently, she spilled coffee onto the table.

Reese sat down opposite her at the small, round table. "Miss Boyce, did you know Harvey was a state trooper?"

Linda shook her head no. "He said he worked for the paper company." She attempted to light a cigarette but could not steady the match. Peck leaned in and held her hand so she could light it. She looked at Peck. "Thank you."

Reese said, "Can you tell me anything else?"

"He liked sex and had the money to pay for it."

Reese and Peck exchanged glances. "He paid you?" Peck said.

Linda looked past Reese at Peck. "This is 1959; don't tell me you never met a hooker before," Linda said.

"I didn't expect one in the middle of nowhere, Dunston Falls," Peck said.

"Wherever there are men," Linda said.

"Let's talk about the intruder," Reese suggested.

"What do you want to know?" The cigarette was doing its job and Linda appeared to be regaining some of her nerve.

"Whatever it is you know and can tell us," Reese said.

Linda puffed on the cigarette and looked Reese in the eyes.

She appeared almost annoyed. "I was talking a bath, he showed up. He hit me on the head. Harvey showed up. He killed Harvey. I called you people. Did I leave anything out?"

Doctor McCoy came in from outside and stood behind Peck. "I got here as soon as I could," McCoy said. He looked at Linda. "Is this her?"

Just after sunrise, Peck and Reese met in the lounge at the hospital. They were drinking coffee and smoking cigarettes when McCoy opened the door and joined them.

McCoy poured coffee into a mug and sat down at the table. "She will sleep most of the day, I'm afraid. In the meantime, do you want an autopsy report on Officer Peterson?"

"For God's sake, doctor. We know what killed him. We need to talk to the girl," Reese said.

"When she's rested," McCoy said. "Otherwise she will be unable to answer your questions to your satisfaction. Why don't you come back later, say around four this afternoon."

"Doctor, we need information," Reese insisted.

"Well, you won't get it from her until around four this afternoon," McCoy said. "Unless gibberish is helpful?"

Reese and Peck found a table at the diner and ordered breakfast. Reese requested his men bring as many dozen eggs, slabs of bacon and potatoes as they could fit into their vans and half the amount went to the diner.

Reese ate his scrambled eggs, bacon and home fries as if it were his last meal. Peck simply picked at his eggs. The appetite wasn't there.

"The natives are growing restless," Peck said.

Reese nodded his agreement as he spooned eggs into his mouth. "They will want answers soon."

"So do I."

"Meaning?"

"You brought all this shit for fingerprints, blood sampling, hair and fiber and I doubt we will extract anything other than Harvey and the woman's prints. Even the bloody footprints belong to the victim."

"Sheriff, you want answers and I don't even know the questions yet," Reese said. "We both know working a homicide takes time, effort and a great deal of luck. Restless or not."

Peck took a sip of coffee and thought a moment. "Answer me this, Lieutenant."

Reese looked over his spoon, giving Peck his full attention.

"I've been here eighteen months and never heard of Linda Boyce until this morning. Harvey was here one day and knew she was a prostitute. Don't you find that a little odd?"

Reese, with a mouthful of eggs stared at Peck. Then Reese slowly chewed and swallowed.

"How did he know that, huh?" Peck said.

Reese set his spoon aside and took a sip of coffee. "My, my, the small town sheriff with the big city question."

"That had to occur to you," Peck said.

"It did," Reese said, nodding his head. "I put it to my men and all they knew was Harvey had a woman stashed away somewhere. He gave no details. To be honest, I am partially responsible for not asking questions when I knew he was sneaking out to meet a woman. The both of us should have known better than to let him get away with it."

"Well, we need more from the girl than that he showed up, Harvey died thing if we're going to catch him before he kills again," Peck said.

"And you're sure that he will?"

"Yes."

"Why?"

"He has the taste for it now."

"Not that I don't agree," Reese said, picking up his spoon. "But last night may have scared him halfway to New Hampshire by now."

"I don't think so."

"Why not?"

"He has forty-seven square miles to hide out in," Peck said.

"And?"

"He likes it here."

Reese spooned some eggs into his mouth and washed them down with coffee. He looked directly at Peck. "Then we better do our job and catch him."

Seven

Late in the day, Peck returned to Linda's hospital room and found her still asleep. He pulled a chair against the wall and sat down. He looked at her in the bed as if seeing her for the first time and realized just how tiny a woman she was. Maybe a hundred and ten pounds soaking wet. He was grateful that she was alive and not just because she did nothing to provoke such a horrible death. She might well turn out to be the key that unlocked the clues that solved the mystery for them. Exhaustion suddenly washed over him and he closed his eyes and was asleep in a matter of minutes.

He woke up an hour later when Linda's voice penetrated his semiconsciousness.

"Sheriff, are you okay?" he heard her say softly.

From his light sleep, Peck heard her voice and he opened his eyes and looked at her in the bed. "Yes." Slightly disoriented, he looked at his watch. "I must have dozed off."

"Where's the other guy, the mean-looking one?"

"Lieutenant Reese?" he said, more awake now.

"I guess so."

Peck stood up to stretch his back. "He's at your house with his team of men."

Linda sat up in bed with her back against the stiff, hospital headboard. "Going through my stuff," she said with mild annoyance.

"It's how you find clues and evidence."

"I suppose," Linda shrugged. "Do you have any cigarettes?"

Peck removed his pack, lit two and gave her one. "It's difficult, but I need you to help me now. I need you to talk me through what happened right up to the end."

Linda blew a smoke ring as she thought. "I never did thank you for being so nice to me, did I?"

"It isn't necessary," Peck said as he retook his seat. "It's my job. So?"

Linda nodded, then said, "I was expecting Harvey around midnight."

"As a client?"

"Yes. Anyway, I started the generator so I could take a bath. When a man is paying you he has the right for you to smell good, and even if he isn't paying you."

"What time was that?"

"Around eleven, eleven-thirty. Right in there somewhere." Linda paused to puff on the cigarette and made eye contact with Peck. "I thought it was Harvey when I heard footsteps. It wasn't."

"What happened then?"

Linda took a deep breath. "It happened so fast. All of a sudden, he was there. He . . . I think it was a log from my woodpile. He hit me with it. In the head. When I woke up, I was tied to the bed. My mouth and eyes were covered in tape. After a little while, he ripped the tape from my eyes, I guess so I could see him."

Peck thought for a moment, and then said, "Did he say anything to you?"

Linda shook her head. "No, nothing."

"Not even one word, nothing?"

"He never made a sound. Never said one word." Linda shook her head again. "He just . . . watched me. Like he was studying me or something. His eyes through the ski mask, they looked yellow."

"Yellow?"

"I know that sounds crazy," Linda said. "I think it was the flame on the candle what made them look that way."

"What happened next?"

Linda took a puff on the cigarette as she looked at Peck. "He . . . I tried to fight, but I couldn't. I couldn't even scream. He had a bread knife from the kitchen. Then . . . he pulled down his pants. He had an erection. The sick bastard is holding a foot-long knife in one hand and his dick in the other. I started to pray he would kill me first."

Linda took another puff on the cigarette and closed her eyes. "Funny the stuff you think when you feel you're going to die. I remember thinking I could stand the pain of the knife, but not of being raped." Linda opened her eyes and puffed on the cigarette.

After a moment of silence, Peck said, "After that what happened?"

"Harvey showed up. I heard his truck and I tried to warn him, but the tape on my mouth . . . I couldn't scream." Linda paused to close her eyes again and take a breath. She opened her eyes and took a sip of water from a glass on the bedside table.

"Take your time," Peck said.

Linda replaced the glass on the table. "Harvey walked in and he was hiding in the shadows behind the door. It happened so fast, I wasn't sure I even saw it. He shoved the knife into Harvey's stomach and Harvey dropped the bottle of scotch he brought for me. He seemed to stand there for a second as if he was admiring what he did, then he was gone and Harvey was on his knees with the knife in his stomach."

"Harvey, he crawled to you and cut you loose," Peck said.

Linda nodded. "He . . . pulled the knife from his stomach first. I can't imagine how much that must have hurt. He saved my life. He said, run to his truck and call for help on the radio."

"Up to that point, you didn't know Harvey was a cop, a state trooper?"

Linda shook her head. "Not until that Lieutenant Reese told me."

Peck thought a moment and said, "There's something I'm not seeing."

Linda smiled for the first time in their conversation. "For twenty bucks you can see a whole lot more."

Peck stood up to toss his cigarette into the toilet. "That reminds me. When this is over, you're under arrest for solicitation, young lady."

Linda wrapped the covers over her shoulders. "It's freezing in here."

Peck reached for the extra blanket in the closet and placed it around her shoulders. "They turn the heat on every two hours. It will warm up."

Linda tucked her arms under the second blanket. "Thank you."

"About Harvey, how did you meet?"

"Like they all do," Linda admitted. "He called me for a date."

"When was that, yesterday?"

Linda shook her head. "No, at least three days ago. He said he got my number from a friend at the paper company. He would not say who because the guy is married. Like that would have mattered. All these married guys and their big secrets." Linda held her cigarette to Peck and he took it and tossed it into the toilet.

"That doesn't make sense," Peck said, returning to the chair.

"What, that the guy is married?"

Peck shook his head. "Harvey called you before the first

murder was even discovered," Peck said. "He was supposedly on duty in Augusta. Why would he do that?"

"Maybe he was horny?" Linda joked.

"Enough to drive two hundred miles and risk his life during a statewide crisis? I haven't been there, but there have to be some women in Augusta who . . . practice your . . . vocation."

"Was Harvey married? He said he was, but he also said he worked for the paper company. A married man will do all kinds of things to keep his wife from finding out," Linda said. "Like the wives care. As long as the man brings the paycheck home and doesn't give her any diseases, most women don't care at all who their husbands are sticking it to. I've heard of some wives joining in for a threesome."

Peck shook that off. "I don't know if Harvey was married but I'll find out from Reese." Peck slumped back in the chair and gently massaged the spot between his eyes just above the nose.

"Do you have a headache?" Linda said, softly.

"I'm working on it," Peck said. "A doozey."

Linda sat up straight in the bed. "I've had those, too." She got out of bed, stood over Peck, and looked at him.

"It starts here," Linda said. She touched the spot between Peck's eyes with one finger. It felt warm and comforting to the touch.

"Then it spreads out." She ran her fingers across his forehead. "Slowly at first."

Peck looked at her as she reached out and touched his face. Her fingers felt warm and sensual against his rough skin and stubble of beard. Peck felt almost embarrassed at the sensation.

"Then, bang," Linda said, suddenly.

Linda placed both hands on the top of Peck's head.

"It's like an explosion went off inside your head."

Peck made eye contact with her and there was an awkward moment of silence. Slowly, Linda lowered her hands. "I can see him," she whispered. "Those yellow eyes looking at me."

Peck stood up and took hold of her hand. It was suddenly freezing. Her arms were covered with goose bumps. "Maybe we better get back to bed." He guided her to the bed and she slipped between the covers.

"If it's we, leave a twenty on the way out," Linda joked. "I have to pay this hospital bill somehow."

Peck returned to the chair and sat.

"It's funny, but I can still taste the glue from the tape in my mouth," Linda said. "I've brushed my teeth a dozen times, but I can still taste it. Maybe it's just my imagination, like a man missing an arm can still feel his fingers."

Peck looked at her and nodded.

"Is there any chance of getting something to eat around here?" Linda said. "Besides medicine and toothpaste?"

"I'll see what I can do," Peck said.

Peck found Doctor McCoy in the small emergency room where he was patching a kid who fell on the ice and bruised his knee.

"The cafeteria open?" Peck said.

"It was. You hungry?"

Peck shook his head. "For Linda Boyce."

"She's awake? Good. I'll check on her."

"Maybe I'll get her something from Deb's," Peck said.

He left the hospital, crossed the street, and entered the diner. Of course, half the town was now aware of the incidents, although details were sketchy. They looked, but the staff and patrons of the diner were respectful and did not push him. Kranston and Regan had made the rounds earlier, stating an official announcement would be forthcoming at Sunday services. That seemed to satisfy their curiosity for the moment.

Peck ordered a cheeseburger with French fries and a large soda to go. The order was ready in fifteen minutes and he carried it back to the hospital in a paper bag.

When Peck entered her hospital room, Linda was not alone. Father Regan had joined her.

"Good evening, Sheriff," Regan said with a smile. "Miss Boyce and I were just having a chat."

"Hello, Father," Peck said.

"Is that food I smell in that bag?" Linda said, sniffing.

"From the diner," Peck said, handing Linda the bag. "It's the best I could do at this hour."

Linda looked into the bag and smiled. "It will do."

"Linda and I were just discussing this Sunday's service," Regan said. "I missed her last week, but she promised to be front row as usual."

Peck looked his question to Linda.

"I was raised Catholic," Linda said as she bit into the cheeseburger.

"And she was about to make the act of confession," Regan said.

Peck, unaware of Regan's hidden request, did not move until the priest cleared his throat and said, "A moment of privacy, Sheriff?"

"Sure, of course," Peck said. He nodded his goodnight to Linda and left the room. In the hallway, he could hear Linda ask the priest if he could wait until after she finished her cheeseburger.

Alone in his office, Peck made a fire in the woodstove, percolated a pot of coffee on its flat service, then sat behind his desk and read reports. There were dozens of statements given by town residents, none of which shed any light on the two murders.

He read Reese's report on Doris White, then his own several times in succession.

The report written on Deb Robertson by Reese was three times as thick as the one on Doris White and he read it through several times with the same results. Nothing. Whatever he was searching for was not there. If it was, it failed to register in his mind.

He read his own report on Deb Robertson, trying hard to differentiate his personal feelings from his professional opinion. It was difficult. Prior to his recent budding relationship, Peck never seriously considered marriage. As he had explained to Deb, there never seemed to be the time to develop the kind of relationship with a woman that would lead to a serious commitment.

That changed in the span of a single evening.

Even though he knew next to nothing about Deborah Ann Robertson, the ease in which they fell into each other's life was a promising start that would be left without a conclusion.

He felt cheated. Then he felt guilty for feeling cheated when Deb was the one lying on a cold slab in the morgue.

As the sheriff in whose jurisdiction her life ended, Peck felt it was his duty to find the man responsible for ending it and to make him pay. As the man who was her final lover, he felt enough internal rage at losing her to rip the sick bastard's head off and stick it on a pole on Main Street.

Neither emotion helped matters and only served to bog down his mind.

Peck read his report a second and third time. He saw nothing that shed any new light upon the growing list of murders. He realized that his feelings for Deb might be clouding his ability to analyze the evidence from an impartial viewpoint. That was a detective's biggest mistake, examining evidence with the heart instead of the head. That was the reason most departments had a policy against a detective investigating crimes committed by relatives or against relatives. To a homicide detective, emotion equated with failure. He remembered seeing some episodes of the TV show *Dragnet.* The two detectives were always deadpan in the way they spoke to suspects or witnesses. Whenever a witness would go off on a tangent, they would always ask for just the facts. It was their way of leaving emotion off the job.

The candles burned low on his desk. His exhausted mind took him nowhere new. He snuffed out the candles, settled in on the cot near the woodstove, and allowed sleep to overcome him.

Peck was sound asleep when something in his subconscious caused him to bolt awake and stare at the black ceiling above his head. He saw something in his sleep that he was missing in his consciousness.

It nagged at him until he stood up, lit a candle and sat behind his desk. Reaching for the bottle of scotch in the drawer, Peck poured an ounce into his empty coffee mug. He lit a cigarette, opened Deb Robertson's file and read it again.

He read the evidence log, which listed all items dusted for fingerprints and tested for blood samples.

There was nothing. He picked up the file for Doris White, read it through again, and finally settled on the evidence log. Then he made a connection, which like most detectives, he missed the first and second time. He read it again and again, then thought about Linda Boyce. That's when he saw it with crystalline clarity, the way a master chess player could see twenty moves down the board.

Closing the Doris White file, Peck stood up, got dressed and left the office.

Behind his desk in the tiny rectory office, Father Regan stifled a yawn as he looked at Peck, who sat in a chair opposite him. The priest appeared disheveled from being awakened from a deep sleep. He also appeared quite grumpy, which was understandable. His thinning hair was matted against his skull and his eyes were red and puffy from lack of sleep.

"Sheriff, what is so important it couldn't wait until morning?" Regan said.

"Tomorrow is Sunday," Peck said.

Regan glanced at the desk clock in front of him. It read two-twenty a.m. "Today is Sunday, Sheriff," he said with mild agitation in his voice.

"And you do mass at what time?"

"Say mass, Sheriff. Mass is always referred to as being said. But to answer your question, it will begin at ten instead of the usual nine due to the circumstances."

"You said Linda Boyce is a regular at your service," Peck said.

"Even prostitutes have souls worth saving, Sheriff."

"Doris White and Deb Robertson were also regulars, is that correct?"

"Yes, but I . . ."

"I missed it the first dozen go rounds," Peck said. "The crucifixes."

"What are you talking about, Sheriff? What crucifixes?"

"The evidence log for both Doris White and Deb Robertson has a crucifix listed among the items. I'd be willing to bet that somewhere in her trailer, Linda Boyce has one as well."

Regan leaned back in his chair and stared at Peck. "You lost me. Maybe you better tell me exactly what's on your mind, Sheriff."

"Have you seen any strange faces at mass recently?" Peck said.

Regan ran his fingers over his mouth as he ingested Peck's question and finally understood. "You're suggesting this madman is using my church to select his victims?"

"Three out of three are regulars," Peck said. "Harvey Peterson was an accident."

"Half the town are regulars. That doesn't make them guilty of anything other than believing in God."

"Half of those believers are female. I'd like to keep that half alive."

Regan nodded his head and ran his fingers across his mouth again, seeing Peck's point and grasping the seriousness of it. "What do you propose?"

When Peck arrived at the logging camp shortly after sunrise, he was pleased to see Reese and his men were early risers. Dressed and ready to roll, they were eating breakfast in the main cabin when he walked in and told Reese he might have something worth listening to if he could spare a cup of coffee.

"I don't know why I didn't catch that," Reese said when Peck was finished. "It's just fucked up enough to be true."

"And possibly to work."

"What are you suggesting, Sheriff?"

"Go to church much, Lieutenant?" Peck said.

From the cramped changing room to the left side of the altar, Peck watched the gathering crowd through a small, tinted window in the door. The church was filling up fast. He wasn't sure if that was Regan's normal flock, or people wanted to hear the news of the murders. Either way, it didn't matter. They were here.

Peck did a quick count of pews and estimated the church would hold two hundred people, not counting standing room in back. He looked at the altar. It was small and common, lacking the intricate designs of a larger, more affluent church and covered in plain, white linen. Large candles burned in plain, six-foot-tall holders on each end of the altar. Centered on the altar rested the communion box, which housed the gold chalice, wine and wafers, used during the ceremony.

Behind him, Regan dressed in a variety of vestment robes he would wear for mass. The priest finished dressing and stood behind Peck to glance through the tinted window. In close quarters, the priest smelled of tobacco.

"It appears I'm needed," Regan said. He opened the door and passed through to the altar.

Peck continued to scan the near capacity crowd through the window. He spotted Reese in a rear pew and several of his men scattered about the various other pews. Even dressed down in plain clothes, they stood out in the crowd. There wasn't anything he could do about it now except hope the regulars were caught up in the mass and didn't notice them.

Regan went to the podium to the left of the altar. "My friends, the generator can provide for heat only. I will try to make my voice heard in back."

Knowing he was not visible through the tinted window, Peck scanned the crowd carefully, paying particular attention to female faces. Since all three women involved had nothing in common as far as looks and personality was concerned, it was impossible to get an understanding of the killer's taste in women, if he even had a particular taste.

Maybe just the fact that the women were religious was enough to set him off on his violent path. Some kind of grudge against God and rage against women. Peck made a mental note to ask Doctor McCoy if he had any psychological reference material on the subject. It might help with a profile.

At the podium, Regan said, "Concerning the deaths of parish members Doris White and Deborah Robertson, pray with me that our almighty God shall keep them in his good graces forever."

Peck continued to scan the crowd as Regan led them in a prayer.

"Bless them our Lord and keep their souls . . ." Regan prayed.

Peck tuned out Regan's prayer and concentrated on the faces of the men in attendance. Many were familiar to him from the hospital and church shelters during the past few days and from the recent interviews. Some he had seen around town during the past year or so and some were completely new to him. Familiar or not, that did not matter. What did matter was anything suspicious he could notice, such as a man paying undue attention toward a woman and not concentrating on the mass.

Suddenly, he spotted a man in the last pew on the left side of the church and zeroed in on him. The man was a mess. His clothing was filthy and his hair was unkempt. A four-day stubble covered his face. But it was the man's eyes which caught Peck's attention. They were out of focus and glazed as if he were high on something. Peck knew that marijuana use had increased since after the war and the youth in the country had little to worry about except the newest rock and roll dance. Maybe the man had managed to get hold of some. Even remote states like Maine were not immune to the rapid changes in the times or culture.

Peck turned away from the window and went to the corner of the room where he removed the walkie-talkie from his utility belt. The radio was massive and heavy and he wished they would modernize police equipment to make it easier to use. Peck keyed the radio and spoke to one of Reese's men outside the church.

"This is Sheriff Peck. Over."

"Go ahead, Sheriff," the man responded. "Over."

"There's a man in the last row on the left side of the church as you enter," Peck said. "I want you to try and get a photograph of him as he leaves the church. He hasn't done anything I could spot, but I don't like the looks of the guy. Over."

"I'll go in and take a peek, make sure I have the right guy and call you back," the man said. "Out."

Peck returned to the window. Reese's man dressed as a civilian entered the church and stood in back. He scanned the last pew and Peck could see his eyes settle on the man. A moment later, he left the church.

Peck's radio crackled to life. "Dirty clothes, unshaven, that the guy? Over."

"That's him. Over," Peck said.

"I'll grab a picture of him, Sheriff. I got a Polaroid in the car. Over."

"You state boys got everything."

"Benefits of the job, Sheriff. Out."

Peck returned his radio to his belt and kept watch through the window. Unlike the other attacks, this one struck without warning. There was no pain or pressure behind the eyes, no headache around the base of his skull. It just hit him like a sledgehammer between the eyes and he found himself on the floor.

Peck reached into his pocket for the prescription pills. He ripped off the cap and swallowed two. He lay as still as possible and waited for the medicine to take effect. In the background, he heard Regan speak from the altar.

"Please rise," the priest said.

Peck curled himself into a tight ball as if forming a shell against the onslaught of pain in his head.

"And recite the Lord's Prayer with me," Regan said.

The pain in Peck's head grew worse. He heard himself say, "Our Father who art in heaven," along with the crowd.

Peck heard Regan say, "Hallowed be thy name."

There was an explosion of color before Peck's eyes as if he were looking through a child's kaleidoscope. He closed his eyes and saw a fireman on a hook and ladder truck as if he were watching a movie. The fireman's face was out of focus and without features. A fire raged all around him as he climbed the ladder to the top.

In the background, Regan said, "Thy will be done, thy kingdom come."

The fireman reached the top of the ladder where a small boy hung out the window of a burning building. The fireman reached for the boy and the boy jumped onto the ladder. The fireman held the boy tightly for a moment, then pointed to something below. As they descended the ladder, a large hunk of debris fell from the building and struck the ladder. The boy, shaken loose, fell screaming to his death. The fireman cried in anguish as he watched the boy reach bottom.

In the background, Regan said, "Now and at the hour of our death. Amen."

As the boy hit the sidewalk below, the vision in Peck's mind suddenly vanished. White spots filled his eyes, then slowly his vision cleared. The pain lessened quickly and in a few minutes was gone.

Peck sat up, then stood up and looked out the tiny window. The crowd inside the church was thinning out quickly. Regan was at the open doors, shaking hands with parishioners. The mass had ended.

Peck turned away and walked to the side door that led to the backyard of the church. An urge overtook him and he leaned over to vomit into a wastebasket.

"Who is he?" Peck asked from behind his desk.

Reese, Bender and Ed Kranston were with him in the office. Reese had several four-by-five, black-and-white photographs of the man from the church, taken with the latest model camera from Polaroid. The camera took photographs that developed a picture within sixty seconds.

"It's the latest thing in police technology," Reese explained for the benefit of Kranston. "I heard that in a few years, the pictures will be in color. The state purchased several of them for homicide units."

Kranston and Bender examined the photograph.

"That's Jonathan Muse," Kranston said, as he inserted a fresh stick of gum into his mouth.

"You know the man?" Peck said.

"Not well," Kranston said. "He's had a rough time paying his property tax. I granted him an extension last year."

Bender looked at the photograph again, then at Peck. "You think he's a suspect?"

"I think he's interesting," Peck said. "Don't you?"

Reese picked up the Polaroid and studied the face of Muse closer. "Yeah, I do."

"Wait," Kranston said. "What makes you think Muse is suspicious? That he came to church looking like a bum?"

Peck turned to Bender. "Jay, you see Muse in town at all since the storm?"

"Come to think of it, no. I haven't seen him in months."

"So he shows up at mass looking like he just stepped out of the Oklahoma dust bowl. Why?" Peck said.

"Maybe he's religious?" Kranston said.

"Maybe," Peck agreed. "Or maybe he's picking out his next victim. Doris White, Deb Robertson and Linda Boyce are all regulars at Sunday mass."

Kranston's eyes went from Bender to Peck to Reese. "Okay, pick him up, but just for questioning. If he's innocent he still has to live here."

"My men and I will do it," Reese said.

"Can I tag along?" Bender said.

Reese nodded and he and Bender left the office.

Kranston said, "You don't want to be in on the action?"

Peck stood up from his desk and reached for his jacket. "The action will come later, after we pick up what might just be nothing more than the town drunk."

Peck walked to the office door.

"Where are you going?" Kranston said.

"To have my head examined."

Peck met McCoy for coffee in the hospital lounge where Peck recanted his nightmarish experience from the church.

"How long did this episode last?" McCoy asked.

"The better part of the ten a.m. mass."

"This dream . . ."

"Not a dream," Peck said. "I was wide awake the entire time. It was like the first time, more a hallucination or vision."

McCoy sipped coffee as he thought for a moment. "I hesitated to bring this up, Dave, but in the past, in the Army, did you experiment with any kinds of drugs?"

"Drugs? What do you mean drugs? Like medicine?"

McCoy shook his head. "More like mind altering drugs. Have you ever heard of LSD?"

"Tom, I don't know what the hell you're talking about."

"I'm glad to hear that and not," McCoy said.

"I don't understand."

"If we eliminate the use of drugs, that's one less possible cause of the problem," McCoy said. "However, that throws an unknown variable into the mix."

"Like?"

"Like I honestly don't know," McCoy said. "That's why it's an unknown variable."

"You sound more like a lawyer than a doctor."

McCoy grinned, then said, "Look, without tests, it's impossible to say what's causing these headaches," McCoy said. "I've read about tumors that . . ."

"Tumors?" Peck said, remembering he thought the exact same thing.

McCoy shook his head. "Dave, that's so remote a possibility, I wouldn't be concerned about it. It just could be plain old stress like we talked about before."

"When will you make that appointment for me?"

"I'll call as soon as the phone lines are up and running."

Peck sighed to himself and looked at McCoy. The doctor showed him a tiny, but reassuring smile.

"I wouldn't worry, Dave," McCoy said. "You're strong as an ox and don't look a day over forty. Whatever is causing these episodes, I'm sure it's nothing to worry about."

Late in the afternoon, Reese and Bender returned with Jonathan Muse in custody. If anything, Muse was even more disheveled than at mass earlier that morning. While Bender sat with Muse in Peck's office, Peck and Reese talked in Kranston's second floor office.

"The man doesn't know which end is up," Reese said. "He didn't even remember going to church this morning."

"Drunk?"

"Not that I could determine. We couldn't find any booze or drugs in what passes for the house he lives in. He must have zero income not to afford the taxes on a shithole like his."

"Did he resist at all?"

"Resist? He couldn't wait to go for a ride," Reese said. "He claimed he hadn't been in a car since Korea."

"So he walked to church from his house?"

"He said he couldn't remember."

"Walking or church?"

"Both walking to church and being in church. The whole morning," Reese said. He paused to look at Peck. "There's something else. The man has a dozen large chef's knives in a kitchen drawer, rope under the sink and a box of latex rubber gloves."

Peck looked at Reese. "I think we should go talk to the man."

In the absence of a conference table per se, they made do with the spare desk in Peck's office. Reese and Peck sat opposite Muse, while Bender sat at his own desk in the background.

Acting as the primary investigator, Reese began the interview. "Mr. Muse, do you have any idea why we asked you to come with us?"

Muse blinked at Reese as if trying to shake the cobwebs from his brain. "I don't even remember who you are or where I am," he said.

"You're at the Dunston Falls police station, Mr. Muse," Reese said. "And I'm Lieutenant Reese of the Maine State Police."

"Why am I here?"

"We asked you to go with us, remember?"

Muse shook his head. "Why?"

"There have been some recent events which need clearing up."

"Events?" Muse looked at Peck and Reese through watery, bloodshot eyes. "What kind of events?"

Peck made eye contact with Muse, searching for something in the fog and haze that reflected back at him that said the man was coherent. "Two women have been murdered. A third nearly murdered and a police officer lost his life saving hers," Peck said.

"So?"

Reese leaned forward and folded his hands on the desk. "So we want to know where you've been the past three days."

Muse shrugged. "Why do you care where I been? I didn't kill them. I didn't kill nobody."

"It would be great if we could just believe everybody at face value, Mr. Muse," Reese said. "But unfortunately, police work doesn't work that way."

"I don't give a rat fuck how it works," Muse said. "Hey, could I have a chocolate bar? I love chocolate bars."

"No," Reese said.

"I saw on the TV once, an episode of *Peter Gunn,*" Muse said. "They were talking to this fellow like you is talking to me now and that fellow asked for a lawyer."

"You don't need a lawyer," Reese said. "You're not under arrest."

Muse stood up. "If I ain't under arrest, I'm going home."

"Sit down, Mr. Muse. I'll get you your chocolate," Peck said.

Bender opened a desk drawer where he removed a chocolate bar and gave it to Peck. "Is this okay?" Peck said, sliding the bar toward Muse.

Muse picked up the bar, ripped off the wrapper and took a bite. He chewed gleefully and smiled at Peck.

"Mr. Muse, we need you to tell us about the last three days," Reese said. "Where you were and what you were doing."

Muse bit off another piece of chocolate. "I think I was home."

"Think?" Reese said.

Muse chewed chocolate and looked at Reese. Muse's confusion was apparent in his eyes. "I ain't sure. I might have gone out for something, a walk, but I don't know. Why, is it important what I was doing?"

"It will help us clear up some missing pieces in our investigation," Reese said.

"Missing pieces? Like what?" Muse said. He munched on the chocolate, seemingly not paying the slightest bit of attention.

Reese glanced at Peck, and then turned to Muse. "Do a lot of cooking, Mr. Muse?"

"Waddaya mean cooking?" Muse said.

"In the kitchen," Reese said. "It's where you prepare your food. You do cook, don't you, Mr. Muse?"

Muse bit off another piece of chocolate as he thought. "Sometimes I cook, when I have food."

"Is that why you have a dozen foot-long kitchen knives?" Reese said.

"I . . . don't know." Muse's eyes appeared even more confused.

"You don't know. It's your kitchen, Mr. Muse," Reese said.

"Then I guess them knives must belong to me," Muse said. His eyes were beginning to glaze over. "You guys are hurting my head."

"What about the rubber gloves and rope under the sink, they belong to you, too?" Reese said.

"I don't know," Muse said. "Probably."

"What do you use them for?" Reese said.

Blood suddenly dripped from Muse's nose. "I'm getting a headache," Muse said and rubbed a spot above his nose.

Peck turned to Bender. "Get a paper towel for Mr. Muse."

Bender reached into his desk for a box of Kleenex, but before he could pass it to Peck, Muse jumped up from his chair and grabbed his head.

"What the hell?" Reese said.

Holding his head, Muse doubled over and gasped for air. "Ah . . . God . . . Help me," he cried.

"Jay, get Doctor McCoy," Peck shouted.

Bender ran from the office.

Reese and Peck stood up. Peck gently touched Muse on the shoulder. "I sent for a doctor, Mr. Muse."

Muse looked up at Peck, gasped loudly, screamed even louder and then his eyes rolled back in his head exposing the whites and he passed out to the floor.

Reese looked at Peck. "Maybe he's allergic to chocolate," Reese said.

Muse was resting comfortably on a bed in the tiny hospital emergency room when Peck and Reese approached McCoy, who was making notes on a chart.

"How is he?" Peck said.

"His vital signs are all normal," McCoy said. "For a man in his mental state and physical condition."

"Which is what?" Peck said.

"I don't know," McCoy confessed. "There's no alcohol in his blood. Drugs, either."

Reese looked at Muse, who appeared sound asleep. "Then what the hell happened to him?"

"My guess would be a migraine. I can't be certain until I run some tests and blood work. Maybe some tests for allergies."

Reese looked at McCoy. "Migraine? You mean a headache?"

"Yes."

"That must have been one hell of a fucking headache," Reese said.

McCoy set the chart on a table and stuck his pen into his shirt pocket. "Most migraines are just that, one hell of a headache."

"When can we resume our interview?" Reese asked.

"He should be fine as soon as he wakes up as long as you don't go bouncing him around too much."

"How long will he be out?" Reese said.

"Four, maybe five hours. I gave him a sedative."

Reese looked at Peck. "I'll go check on my men, see if they made any progress. Care to tag along, Sheriff?"

"Go ahead. I want to talk to the doctor."

In the lounge, Peck and McCoy drank coffee as they sat at the table. Several candles provided enough light for McCoy to write on a chart.

"That man is so confused he doesn't know whether to wind his ass or scratch his watch," Peck said, which drew a smile from McCoy.

A generator suddenly came on and the lights flickered to life. McCoy blew out the candles.

"Is it because of the headaches?" Peck said.

"That could be. Migraines can be very disorienting as you found out. I've been doing some reading. Some people report they see a tunnel with blue light. Others claim hallucinations."

Peck lit a cigarette and studied McCoy for a moment. "Linda Boyce told me she has these headaches. She also said the man who murdered Peterson looked to her as if he also had a headache. Now Muse."

"I'm not following you, Dave. What's your point?"

"What are the odds there are four of us suffering migraines in a town this size at the same time?"

"Actually, I would say they're about normal," McCoy said. "The 1958 report from the Surgeon General's office stated that about three percent of the American public suffers from migraines. That would make some nine people in our town suffering the same as you are. Small consolation if you're one of the nine."

Peck stared at McCoy.

McCoy smiled. "Dave, I want you to take it easy for a few days. Maybe you should back off and let Reese handle things. Spend a few days at home doing nothing and thinking about nothing. More than your body, your mind needs a rest."

"Go home and do nothing while a murderer runs loose?"

"One day then. Just one good night's sleep in your own bed away from the office," McCoy insisted, "might be just what you need."

"Maybe you're right," Peck said. "Sleeping in my own bed sounds like a pretty good idea." Peck stood up from the table and turned to the lounge door where he paused. "As long as I'm here, is it okay if I look in on the Boyce woman?"

"It's okay, except she isn't here," McCoy said. "She was fit enough so Lieutenant Reese had her moved to the logging camp for her own protection."

"Yes, that's the smart move," Peck said and opened the door. He paused to look at the doctor. "Say Tom, let's keep these headaches between us for now."

"You're my patient, Dave," McCoy said. "I couldn't reveal your medical records without a court order, anyway."

Peck nodded, exited the lounge and closed the door behind him.

Kranston was behind his desk when Peck entered the town manager's office after leaving the hospital. As Peck approached his desk, Kranston glanced up from the document he was writing on and acknowledged Peck with a slight head nod.

"I'm usually not here this late," Kranston said, shuffling a mound of paper in front of him. "But with everything that's happened, I've fallen behind."

Peck walked to the chair opposite Kranston's desk and sat down. "I need to talk to you, Ed."

Kranston glanced up at Peck. "Sure, Dave. Just give me a moment to sign off on this."

Peck watched Kranston stack papers into a folder. Holding the folder Kranston said, "What did you want to talk to me about?"

"Me."

Flipping the folder closed, Kranston said, "You? I don't understand."

"There's no other way to say it, so I'll come right to the

point," Peck said. "I'm no longer fit to be the chief law enforcement agent for your town."

Kranston quit fooling with his papers and gave Peck his undivided attention. "What are . . . I don't understand. What are you saying?"

"I have reasons I'd rather not go into just yet," Peck said. "But I can no longer serve as sheriff of Dunston Falls."

Kranston stared at Peck for several seconds before responding. "What the hell does that mean, reasons? What reasons? Is it these murders? Because if it is, I'll assume responsibility for the delay in . . ."

"It isn't the murders, Ed. Not directly, anyway. It's me. I have a possible medical condition which might make it dangerous for me to continue with my duties."

"A dangerous medical condition? I don't understand. What does that mean?"

"Just what it sounds like, Ed. Continuing with my duties could pose a danger to myself and others. That's all I can say right now."

"I'm shocked, Dave," Kranston said. "Stunned. I don't know what to say." He slid open the top drawer of the desk and removed a pack of gum. "Have you discussed this with Doctor McCoy?"

"Yes."

"And what did he say?" Kranston said as he removed the wrapper from a stick of gum and placed it into his mouth.

"He's recommended I see a specialist as soon as the phones are back and he can call Maine Medical Center."

"I see. This is so sudden I don't know what to say."

"There's nothing to say, Ed," Peck said. "Reese is a good man and he will catch this guy. Jay has come a long way and will make a fine sheriff. I'll stay on until my appointment at the hospital and help Jay get acclimated."

Kranston nodded his head at Peck and stood up to shake his hand.

"If it's all right with you, I'd like to tell Jay myself," Peck said.

"Of course," Kranston said.

Peck turned and walked to the door and opened it. "Good night, Ed," Peck said and exited the office.

Still standing, Kranston stared at the door until the closet door in the far corner of his office opened and McCoy stepped out. As McCoy approached the desk, Kranston lowered himself to his seat and opened a second stick of gum.

"We have a problem," McCoy said. "A big fucking problem."

Kranston looked up at McCoy and stuck the second piece of gum into his mouth. "Yes, we do."

"How do we handle it?"

"We wait."

"Not for too long, I hope."

"How long is too long?" Kranston said.

McCoy lowered himself into the chair vacated by Peck and silently made eye contact with Kranston.

"Because I don't know what that is anymore," Kranston said.

Eight

With a glass of scotch and a cigarette for company, Peck sat on his sofa for the first time since the ice storm began. A fire crackled loudly in the woodstove, warming the living room. Several candles burned on the coffee table, illuminating the living room with dim, iridescent light.

Lost in thought, Peck was not aware the full moon rose earlier until he noticed its bright light cascading through the living room window. He stood from the sofa and walked to the window to look out. Brightly lit snow fell gently to the ground, reflecting so much moonlight you could almost read by it. He thought the scene looked perfect in its simplicity and felt beckoned by it. With a sudden desire to feel the cold, crisp night air, he opened the window and filled his lungs. Never had he smelled anything as sweet, as crisp and invigorating.

Turning away from the window, Peck grabbed his jacket, gloves and wool hat.

Peck found a quiet bliss in riding a snowmobile through the moonlit woods without purpose or direction. The ride did not involve police work or destination and he took the midnight run just for the sheer enjoyment of the experience. Even the loud roar of the snowmobile engine seemed to fade into the background.

He crossed a frozen stream and slowed to a stop near a thicket of trees. He dismounted, removed his helmet and lit a cigarette. Snow fell gently all around him and all sound was lost to the ear in the cushion of nature. He felt at ease and relaxed for the first time since the storm. Maybe McCoy was right, that the stress was building up to a boil and he needed a night of relaxation.

Three hundred yards to Peck's immediate left, the man in the ski mask walked through two feet of snow to a snowmobile parked behind a giant pine tree. He paused for a moment to listen to the stillness around him. Sound traveled extremely well at night and he thought he heard something. He reached for a rifle that was strapped to the snowmobile in a side holster.

The rifle was a bolt action 7MM with a scope and he threw the bolt to chamber a round, and then raised the rifle to his shoulder. As he peered through the scope, the man in the ski mask scanned the woods and spotted Peck. Seen through the cross hairs, Peck tossed his cigarette into the snow, and then mounted his snowmobile.

Just before Peck started the snowmobile, he hesitated and peered into the surrounding woods as if searching for something.

The man in the ski mask lined up Peck's face in the cross hairs of the scope. He watched Peck stare into the woods and his finger tightened around the trigger. As the man in the ski mask was about to pull the trigger, Peck's face suddenly relaxed and he started the snowmobile.

The man in the ski mask watched Peck drive away on his snowmobile, then lowered the rifle. There would be other days.

Peck found himself traveling on a snow-covered dirt road not far from the logging camp. At a clearing on a hill that overlooked the camp, he slowed to a stop and dismounted.

From a saddlebag, Peck removed a thermos and filled the cap with hot coffee. He lit a cigarette and leaned against the snowmobile to enjoy the quiet of the moment. Snow fell lightly around him and the stillness in the woods had a magical effect on his stress-filled mind. As he sipped from the thermos cap, Peck felt the tension melt from his neck and back and shoulders. All at once, he felt at ease.

Off in the distance, something suddenly caught Peck's eye. Unable to make out what it was, he moved away from the snowmobile and peered through the darkness. There was something, but he couldn't tell what. He turned the handlebars of the snowmobile, aimed its powerful headlight and clicked it on.

Peck set the thermos cap on the snowmobile seat and stared into the beam of the headlight. Something in the distance caught the light and reflected it back to him.

"What the hell . . . ?" Peck said to himself.

Slowly, Peck started walking away from the snowmobile. After just thirty feet, he stood in two feet of fresh snow. His eyes followed the beam of light from the snowmobile headlight.

Something was out there, but he couldn't tell what it was from this distance. Walking toward it, there was no way to judge just how far away the something was. He broke into a slow, clumsy jog. After a hundred yards, his legs burned from the effort of trudging through knee-deep snow. He paused to catch his breath, and then continued.

As he got closer, the terrain became a steep hill and running through the snow became more and more difficult. He slipped and fell, but bounced back up and continued with ice and snow stuck to his face and jacket.

After six hundred yards, Peck gasped for air. His lungs were on fire and his legs were cramping badly, but he refused to stop. For some unknown reason, he had to see whatever that was in the beam of light.

He fell again and used it as an excuse to catch his breath. As he lay on his stomach, Peck peered into the beam of light and thought his imagination had run wild. Several hundred yards away there appeared to be a wall of brightly gleaming silver.

Peck stood up and started walking. He quickly broke into a run again and forced his body to make the final two hundred yards.

At the top of the hill, Peck came to a sudden stop. Fifteen feet directly in front of him was a twelve-foot-high, chain-link fence. Was he hallucinating again? He walked, then ran to the fence and grabbed it with gloved hands. It was real. He looked left and then right and the fence extended as far as his eyes could see. It glistened with snow and ice as it reflected the beam of light from his snowmobile.

Peck stepped back, turned around and sat in the snow with his back against the fence. He searched his memory, visualizing the map behind his desk. There were no markings on the map for fence lines that he could remember. Could the paper company have erected the fence to protect its land? No, that didn't make sense. Protect it from what? There was nothing out there, not even a road.

The questions racing through his mind were what the fence was doing here and who installed it?

He stood up and felt his legs cramp. Another thought popped into his mind, what purpose did it serve?

Peck dismounted his snowmobile on a high ridge, which overlooked the logging camp and looked down upon the main cabin. The small sleeping cabins were dark and quiet, but light shone in the windows of the main hall. In the moonlight, smoke rose from its chimney and appeared like a bright silver band rising to the clouds. The aroma of the burning wood carried to him on the light winter breeze.

Peck slowly descended the ridge and stayed in shadows as he

entered the camp. There were a half dozen vehicles parked around the main hall, one of which Peck recognized immediately as McCoy's ambulance.

Bewildered, Peck crept to the side of the main hall and paused at a window to peer inside. He could see well enough, but the thick glass muffled the voices.

Reese and several of his men stood in front of the sofa that faced the fireplace and looked at Linda Boyce. Dressed in pajamas and a white robe, Linda sat on the sofa and appeared to stare into space. Her eyes were glazed over, her breathing sounded labored and nasal as if she had a cold.

Suddenly, there was the sound of a toilet flushing and McCoy exited the bathroom and walked toward Linda. He reached for the penlight in his shirt pocket and shone it directly into Linda's eyes.

"Not good," McCoy said, lowering the penlight.

"What," Reese said, "is not good?"

"We're losing her," McCoy said, looking at Reese.

"What the hell does that mean?"

McCoy sighed loudly. "I asked for Peck. Where is he?"

Reese glared at McCoy. "You said he would be at home. He was not. My men are looking for him right now."

McCoy felt Linda's face, and then rolled up one eyelid to inspect her pupils. "You fucking CIA are all the same."

"Don't lay blame on me, doctor," Reese said. "If you'd let me place the transmitter under his skin like I wanted to, we'd know exactly where he is at all times."

"And if he found that transmitter, what then?" McCoy snapped. "Don't you think he might be just a bit curious as to what a micro-transmitting device was doing in his neck?"

Reese bit his tongue and remained silent.

"Have you told Kranston?" McCoy said.

"No need," Reese reassured McCoy. "We'll find him before he has a need to know."

"You better."

Linda moaned and her head slumped to her chest.

"Take her back to her cabin and have a man stay with her," McCoy said. "Make sure she stays warm, but if a fever comes on, call me immediately."

Reese looked at two of his men and they moved to the sofa.

Peck flattened himself against the side of the main hall as McCoy opened the front door and stepped outside.

"You better find him tonight, Mr. CIA," McCoy said to somebody inside the house, then entered the ambulance.

Peck moved slowly to the front of the main hall and watched as McCoy started the engine and drove away.

Peck was about to step out from the shadows when the door opened again and two men and Linda Boyce appeared in the doorway of the main cabin. Linda had an arm draped around each man's shoulder as if unable to walk on her own. They more dragged her than anything else until they reached her cabin and went inside.

Peck turned away, crept to the rear of the main hall and ascended the ridge where he disappeared into darkness. At the top of the ridge, he sat on the snowmobile and mulled it all over in his mind, trying to understand what he had just witnessed.

A hundred feet from his house, Peck stood behind a tree and stared at his house. He was invisible, cloaked in darkness, but he turned away and cupped his hands to light a cigarette. Even a tiny flame could be seen at a great distance after dark.

He lowered himself to sit with his back to the tree and smoked the cigarette. He was confused about the entire night, the fence, McCoy and Reese at the main hall and especially Linda Boyce. She appeared drugged, maybe sedated. He had no idea what was going on around him, but instinctively, he knew some of the answers lay inside his own house.

Peck tucked the spent cigarette into the snow, then stood up and faced his house. He came out of the shadows and slowly walked to the rear of his house where he peered through the glass window on the rear door.

A shadowed figure sat on the sofa. The figure was motionless as if waiting for something. Peck realized the something was himself. He slowly backed away from the door and worked the situation around in his mind, searching for his next move.

Inside Peck's house, the lone figure sat on the sofa in the dark and waited. The quiet was suddenly shattered when the deafening roar of a snowmobile sounded from outside the house. As he jumped up from the sofa and ran to the window, there was a loud crash. He reached the window and pulled back the drapes. "Shit," he yelled as the powerful light of the stalled snowmobile blinded him.

At that moment, Peck kicked in the rear door and aimed his .357 revolver at the shadowed figure. "Don't you move," Peck shouted.

The figure, a semiautomatic pistol in his right hand, turned around to face Peck.

"Drop the weapon," Peck shouted.

The figure dropped the pistol and stepped forward out of the shadows.

"Jay?" Peck said in complete shock when he saw the figure was his deputy.

Bender smiled at Peck as he took a step toward Peck. "Hello, Dave."

"What are you doing in my house?" Peck said.

"I'm waiting, Dave," Bender said calmly and took another step forward.

"Waiting for what, and don't you move!" Peck said.

"For you, Dave. I'm waiting for you," Bender said in his youthful, friendly voice.

Peck squinted at Bender. "Why?"

Bender inched closer to Peck. "Why do you think?"

"I don't know what to think," Peck said. "And that's close enough."

"Are you going to shoot me?" Bender said, smiling his boyish grin. "Look, another woman's been attacked. Reese asked me to bring you to the logging camp. He said we need to hurry."

"What for?"

"I just said another woman's been attacked. That's all I know."

"What's her name?"

Bender shrugged. "I just said, I don't know. She's with Doctor McCoy at the hospital."

"Really," Peck said. "That's funny, because I just left the logging camp where McCoy was busy examining Linda Boyce and shouting orders at Reese like a junior Adolph."

"I don't know what you're talking about, Dave," Bender said. The smile was gone now. "All I know is I'm supposed to wait for you."

"Well, here I am," Peck said. "The waiting is over."

Bender inched forward again, which did not go unnoticed by Peck.

"That's far enough, Jay," Peck said.

"Sure, whatever you say, Dave. Look, could you put the gun down. It's making me nervous."

"Pretend it isn't there."

"It's pointing right at me," Bender said, pointing to Peck's revolver. "What if it goes off by mistake?"

"That would be an unfortunate accident." Peck squinted at

Bender's face. "Are you CIA like Reese?"

"I don't know what that is."

"Reese does," Peck said. "Let's ask him."

Bender took a full step toward Peck. Less than six feet separated the two men.

"I told you not to move," Peck shouted.

Bender paused and smiled at Peck.

"Is something funny?" Peck asked.

In a swift and startling move, Bender performed a perfectly timed karate sidekick and knocked the gun from Peck's hand. Startled, Peck didn't move.

"Now we can talk," Bender said, posturing greatly as he lowered his leg.

Peck stared at Bender, with a where-the-hell-did-that-come-from expression on his face.

"Why don't we have a seat on the sofa, Dave," Bender said.

Without hesitation, Peck charged Bender like a linebacker and attempted to bring him down. Bender moved quickly, caught Peck just under the shoulder and used his own weight to toss Peck on his back to the floor in a perfectly timed Judo move.

"Don't fight me, Dave," Bender said and kicked Peck in the ribs. "You can't win and I'll just have to fuck you up. Just let me take you in quietly." The friendly tone was gone from Bender's voice, replaced by a deeper, more ominous one.

Peck looked up at Bender. "In? In where?"

"Just in, Dave. That's all you need to know." Bender reached for his handcuffs. "Now let's do this quietly."

As Bender grabbed Peck's right arm, Peck slammed his body into Bender and they spilled to the floor. Peck landed on top and got off several good blows to Bender's face before Bender struck Peck in the head with his right foot, knocking Peck sideways to the floor.

Bender jumped to his feet. "I said quietly, you stupid, fucking asshole," Bender shouted. He wiped blood from his nose onto his pants. "Goddammit."

Peck attempted to roll over, but Bender kicked him a half dozen times in the ribs. "Jesus Christ, you're thick headed!" Bender shouted.

Checking his anger, Bender stepped back and wiped blood from his lip. "Look at this," he said, rubbing the blood on his shirt. "Son of a bitch."

Face down on the floor, Peck spied his revolver and inched toward it.

"Where are you going?" Bender laughed.

Peck reached toward the revolver with his left hand.

"Oh, you want that, do you?" Bender said.

Bender reached down and took hold of Peck by the hair. As Bender yanked Peck backward, Peck took him completely off guard when he spun and delivered a vicious right hook to Bender's exposed groin.

There was a freeze frame second before the pain in Bender's testicles kicked in. Then, in a reflex action, Bender lowered his hands and covered his genitals as he gasped and slowly sunk to his knees. "Goddamn you," he hissed through the pain.

Peck jumped up and threw a perfectly timed left hook to Bender's exposed jaw, knocking him to the floor. Then, following Bender's lead, Peck kicked his deputy several times in the ribs and stomach.

Breathing hard, Peck stepped back and looked around for his revolver, spotted it on the floor and went to pick it up. As he turned around, Bender had pulled a second pistol from an ankle holster and racked the slide.

Peck and Bender stared at each other as Bender slowly made his way to his feet. Bender grinned and spit blood. "The moment of truth, Dave," Bender said. He spit again and a broken tooth hit the floor. "That's a pretty good left hook you have. I think you busted my jaw."

"Want to see it again?" Peck said.

Bender shook his head. "Unfortunately, we're out of time."

With the revolver by his side, Peck cocked the hammer.

"Out of time for what?"

Bender and Peck made eye contact and Peck thought he saw a tiny grin in Bender's eyes as the man pulled the trigger of his pistol. A split second later, Peck fired his revolver.

Bender's pistol jammed and misfired. Peck's revolver did not.

Bender dropped the pistol and grabbed hold of his throat on the left side where Peck's bullet entered. Blood literally gushed from the wound. Astonishment showed in Bender's eyes as he looked at Peck in disbelief at having been shot. A moment later, he fell dead to the floor.

NINE

Peck raced the snowmobile at top speed for as long as its engine would hold together. When it started to smoke, he slowed to a crawl, then finally stopped near a grove in the woods to allow the engine to cool.

Peck dismounted and paced in circles through two feet of snow, wondering what the fuck just happened. In twenty-seven years on the job, he never fired a shot he could remember. Now he just blew his own deputy away. In the blink of an eye, Jay Bender was no longer among the living.

He could see him still in his mind's eye. The incredulous expression on Bender's face when he realized a bullet entered his neck. There was that split second before the blood exploded from the wound. Finally, there was the look of understanding in Bender's eyes that he knew in a moment he would be dead and that there was nothing he could do to prevent it from happening.

It was over so fast there was no time to think or react to the situation.

Now it began to sink in. He had actually killed a man. His own man.

A few feet from the snowmobile, Peck sunk to his knees where he began to sob. Once the floodgates opened, he could not shut it off. He cried until the muscles in his stomach ached and still he could not stop himself. Finally, there were no more tears and he stood up and faced the snowmobile. Mounting it, Peck started the cooled engine and continued along the path.

The moon was low across the sky as Peck approached the rear door of the hospital on foot. He lost his watch in the fight with Bender, but he put the time at around three a.m.

Trying the door, he found it locked. Not willing to chance an encounter with a stray town resident up for the night, Peck used his utility knife to pry open the door.

The dark hallway led to the private quarters of Doctor McCoy. Lighting a match, Peck walked the hallway and stopped in front of McCoy's bedroom door. Peck tried the knob and found it unlocked. He blew out the match and stepped inside. He lit another match, spotted a candle on the dresser and lit that.

McCoy was asleep in bed.

Peck stood over the sleeping doctor, and then quickly cupped his hand over McCoy's mouth. McCoy awoke with a panicked start.

"You been looking for me, Tom," Peck said. "Well, here I am."

Wide-eyed, McCoy stared at Peck and muffled something through Peck's hand. Peck removed his hand and McCoy quickly sat up in bed. "What the hell do you think you're doing?"

"Saving you the trouble of hunting me down," Peck said.

"Hunting . . . what are you talking about?"

"Cut the crap, Tom. I've had a rough night."

"What . . . where's Bender?"

"You mean my deputy?" Peck said. "The last time I saw him he was on the floor of my living room not looking so good from the bullet I put in his neck."

"You . . . killed him?"

Peck nodded. "He didn't give me a choice."

"Oh my God," McCoy said as he swung his legs off the bed to stand.

"Careful, Tom," Peck said and patted the .357 revolver in his holster.

"No need for that, Dave," McCoy said. "I just want to examine you."

"No more examinations, Tom," Peck said. "No more bullshit. Tell me what's going on around here and I mean now."

"You're suffering a breakdown, Dave," McCoy said, calmly. "That's what's going on."

Peck smacked McCoy across the face with the back of his right hand. The blow produced a cracking sound and spun McCoy's head around. "I said no more bullshit."

McCoy rubbed his cheek and looked at Peck. "Jesus Christ, look at you, Dave. You need help. You need a specialist. Somebody more qualified than me."

"What for, Tom? What's a specialist going to do for me now?"

"What for, you said?" McCoy said. "How about the likelihood of a brain tumor, that is what for. Because that's what I think you have and only a specialist is qualified to make that determination and treat it before it kills you."

"Like the way you treated Linda Boyce, Tom?"

"What? I don't understand. What about Linda Boyce?"

"I was at the logging camp. I saw you examine her. I heard you bark orders at Reese as if he was a junkyard dog. You called him Mr. CIA."

McCoy attempted to stand, but Peck shoved him back to the bed. "Would you listen to yourself, Dave?" McCoy said. "CIA. What in the hell is that? You have classic paranoia. It's a symptom of a complete nervous breakdown."

"Bender tried to shoot me in my own house, Tom," Peck said. "What's that a symptom of?"

"You need help, Dave. A great deal of help."

"Get dressed."

McCoy looked at Peck, but remained motionless.

"Then don't get dressed. Let's go."

"Go where?"

"To get some answers."

"Answers to what?" McCoy said. "I don't even have the questions."

"Then what good are you?"

Peck pulled his revolver and smacked McCoy across the face with it. As metal struck skull, there was a dull thud and McCoy fell backwards to the bed. Grabbing a pillow, Peck smothered McCoy's face with it, stuck the revolver against the pillow and pressed his knee against McCoy's chest.

"Goodbye, Tom," Peck said.

"Wait. Stop. Hold on a minute," McCoy shouted through the pillow. "Think what you're doing for God's sake."

"What am I doing, Tom?" Peck cocked the hammer on the revolver. "Because I just don't know anymore."

"Jesus Christ," McCoy cried.

"Answers. Who has them?" Peck said.

"Kranston. He's the only one."

Peck removed the pillow from McCoy's face and de-cocked the hammer on the revolver. A large mark from the revolver glowed red on the side of McCoy's face.

"But he won't tell you anything," McCoy said.

"Why?"

McCoy hesitated, then said, "Because the answers might kill you, that's why."

Peck motioned with the revolver. "Get dressed."

Suddenly, from outside the bedroom, the sound of an approaching car filtered through the bedroom door. The engine shut down and a car door opened.

Peck looked at McCoy. "Expecting company?"

McCoy jumped off the bed. "Help," he screamed. "In here."

Peck smacked the revolver against McCoy's face again, knocking him to the floor. "Hush," Peck said.

Peck stood behind the door and waited. The door opened and two of Reese's men cautiously entered. They spotted McCoy on the floor and rushed to him. Peck jumped out from behind the door, struck one man in the face with the revolver and clubbed the second man over the head. They fell unconscious to the floor near McCoy's bed.

"No time to get dressed now," Peck said and yanked McCoy to his feet. "Let's go. Move."

Bleeding from the nose and mouth, McCoy looked at Peck. "Go? Go where?"

From a hundred yards deep in the woods, Peck and McCoy lay in the snow and watched the scene unfold at Peck's house. The activity was near chaotic.

An ambulance and two cars were parked along the dirt road directly in front of the house. Several men in Army uniforms stood around and smoked cigarettes, seemingly unsure of what to do. Two men in white coats carried Bender out on a stretcher and loaded him into the ambulance.

Watching Peck's house, wearing only pajamas and bedroom slippers, McCoy shivered against the snow. "I'm fucking freezing, Dave."

"Shut up," Peck snapped.

"I'm in my goddamn pajamas. My feet are getting frostbite."

"I told you to get dressed." Peck turned to look at McCoy's feet. "Now shut up or I'll shut you up. Which?"

Peck watched the two men in white coats slam the ambulance doors closed and wave to the soldiers as they boarded the ambulance.

"Am I imagining that, Tom?" Peck said. "Those soldiers and

that ambulance, is that my imagination run wild?"

"No, they're there," McCoy admitted. "Because those are National Guard called up by the governor at your request. That ambulance also appears to be courtesy of the Guard as well."

Peck turned to look at McCoy.

"That's right, Dave. You would know that if you were not running around the woods all night, playing John Wayne."

In spite of the frigid temperature, Peck began to sweat. "Bender attacked me. He knew things, martial arts. He said he was there to take me in."

"Bender was in the Army, like you. They teach that stuff in the Army, don't they?"

"No," Peck said. "You're lying. I saw you shout orders at Reese. You called him CIA after you examined Linda Boyce."

"Are you sure? Are you positive?"

Peck wiped sweat from his face as he stared at his house. "No. I mean yes, I am positive. You're trying to confuse me and it won't work."

McCoy said, "Linda Boyce is a diabetic. Reese was supposed to make sure she got her insulin shot. He did not. She was going into shock. Did I yell at him? You bet your ass I did. He almost killed her with his incompetence, the fool."

Struggling to breathe, feeling as if his lungs were filling with water, Peck felt a twinge of pain between his eyes. He reached into a pocket for the pills, opened the cap and swallowed three. He looked at McCoy. "You called Reese CIA. I heard you."

"You heard me through a wall from how far away?"

Peck grabbed McCoy by the pajama shirt and pulled him close. "Bullshit. I heard you. Mr. CIA you called him."

"Are you going to beat me up again?" McCoy said. "Is that your new style, roughing up doctors who are trying to help you?"

Peck looked at his hand on McCoy' pajama shirt, then

pushed the doctor away. "I heard you," Peck said. "I don't care what you say, I heard you."

An Army jeep unexpectedly arrived at Peck's house with two additional soldiers. They joined the first two soldiers and engaged in a heated discussion as if trying to reach some sort of decision.

"See that, Tom? Those are reinforcements. Why would that be necessary if what you're saying is true?"

"Oh, I don't know. Maybe because you're running around the woods killing people," McCoy said.

"I don't think so," Peck said. He stared at the soldiers. One of them pointed to the tracks Peck made earlier when he drove his snowmobile up the front porch. "You said Kranston's answers would kill me. What did you mean by that?" The soldiers traced the second set of snowmobile tracks Peck made earlier when he left his house.

McCoy failed to respond and after several seconds, Peck turned to discover the doctor had vanished. Peck had underestimated McCoy's resiliency and the man had taken advantage of his momentary distraction and run off.

Suddenly, McCoy emerged from the woods near the soldiers. McCoy grabbed a soldier and pointed to the woods, directly at Peck.

"Shit," Peck said.

As the soldiers took off in his direction, Peck stood up from behind the tree and ran deeper into the woods where the snowmobile was parked.

When he finally slowed the snowmobile to a stop in a clearing, Peck had no idea if he was still within the boundaries of Dunston Falls. The fence he encountered earlier might not skirt the entire property line. He might have stumbled upon an opening and driven through it. He could be in Canada or New Hampshire for all he knew. Either way, it did not matter.

What did matter was that he had to find shelter, safety and food.

Peck dismounted the snowmobile and smoked a cigarette as the sun rose. He could hardly believe it when at first light he spotted an old cabin a hundred yards directly in front of him.

Peck drove the snowmobile as close to the cabin as possible, then walked the remaining ten feet through waist-high snow to the front door.

The door fell inward simply by leaning on it. Peck entered the one-room cabin and looked around. Hunters had abandoned the cabin many years ago, was his guess.

A rickety table with two chairs occupied the center of the one room. The sink was a wood box with a hand pump, rusted solid. A double bed with springs showing through the mattress sat against the wall under a window. A corroded woodstove took up the corner opposite the bed. Peck inspected the stove and it wasn't airtight, but still capable of holding a fire. Its stovepipe chimney rose up to the ceiling where it poked through.

Returning to the snowmobile, Peck drove it to the rear of the cabin and hid it in a snowdrift. There was half a thermos of coffee left in the saddlebag and he brought it inside the cabin.

Sipping coffee, Peck sat in a chair and smoked a cigarette. Exhaustion began to seep into his body and slow his thought process. He needed to sleep.

Standing, Peck took a chair and smashed it on the floor. He placed the broken pieces of wood into the woodstove, and then searched the cabin for some kind of starter. He found dozens of old newspapers in a drawer next to what used to be a sink, crinkled some of them and stuffed them into the woodstove. He lit the newspaper with his lighter. It burned quickly, the fire took hold, and the chair pieces burned.

After replacing the door, the tiny cabin was nearly airtight and it warmed within minutes.

Drained of all energy, Peck lay down on the lumpy old bed, positioned himself in such a way as to avoid the mattress springs and was asleep within seconds.

Night had fallen by the time Peck stirred on the bed. He awoke, stood up and stretched the kinks from his back. He was beginning to feel his age, which at that moment felt more like eighty-three than fifty-three.

Outside the cabin, Peck could hear the winds of a new storm approaching. He peeked through the door and fresh snow was falling. His tracks were already covered. If they were searching for him, and Peck was sure that they were, it would be impossible to trail him to the cabin. They would have to wait out the storm, which bought him additional time. But, time to do what?

Peck used more of the old newspapers to start another fire made from the second chair. As the cabin warmed, he searched the drawers and cabinets above and below the old sink and discovered four unopened cans of baked beans. Hidden in an old coffee can under the sink, Peck found a sealed pint bottle of bourbon.

Using the utility knife on his belt, Peck opened a can of beans and set it on the fire to heat. He sat on the bed, cracked the seal on the bourbon and took a thirsty swallow. The liquor immediately heated his stomach. After a second swallow, the warmth spread to his entire body. Carefully, he poured a small amount of bourbon into the open can of beans.

He lit a cigarette. Okay, so he would not starve or freeze to death in the immediate future. That was not nearly good enough. He needed food, supplies, and most of all answers.

As Peck thought, the can of beans bubbled over on the woodstove. He removed it and used the utility knife to spoon beans into his mouth. He washed the meal down with several more hits of bourbon.

The snow was falling harder when he left the cabin and mounted the snowmobile. There was half a tank of gas left and he needed more fuel. He decided to go shopping.

At the intersection of a fire road deep into the woods, Peck shut down the engine and sat still for several seconds, straining his hearing. Sound traveled exceptionally well at night and even better when it snowed. In the far distance, he heard the rumbling of snowmobile engines.

They were looking for him.

Peck started the engine and drove along the fire road until he spotted a small house set back off the road. He parked the snowmobile several hundred feet from the house and stayed along the tree line as he approached it on foot.

The house was dark and quiet. Its residents were probably still in town at one of the shelters. Peck went to the front door and found it unlocked. He entered, using his flashlight to guide him into the house where he searched the rooms on the first floor. Nobody was home. There was a spiral staircase adjacent to the living room, which probably led to a second floor, master bedroom. He skipped searching the second floor and went directly to the kitchen.

The cabinets were full of canned goods, bottled water and packaged foods. Hidden below the sink, wrapped in a towel, was a carton of cigarettes. Peck ripped the curtains off a kitchen window and loaded as much as he could fit onto the material and tied it into a knot. As an afterthought, he took four packs of cigarettes from the carton. They weren't his brand, but they would do.

Peck was about to exit the house and search the shed out back for gasoline when he heard a noise from the second floor. He paused, waited and heard it again. He strained his hearing, still unsure of what the noise was, but it sounded like a footstep.

Peck set the sack of goods on the floor and drew his revolver. He approached the spiral staircase and slowly, silently ascended it. At the top of the landing was a single door and it was closed. Peck replaced the flashlight into his belt and stood close to the door to listen.

There was the sound of breathing, labored and strained as if someone were struggling desperately to breathe.

He looked down to the bottom of the door and flickering light reflected on the wood floor. The light of a candle, he guessed. Grabbing his flashlight, Peck took hold of the doorknob, counted to three and shoved open the door.

A naked woman, tied with rope to the bed, jumped as Peck entered the bedroom. Her mouth, bound with duct tape muffled her scream. As Peck took a step toward the bed, she signaled him with her eyes.

Peck spun around a second too late and the man in the ski mask smashed the revolver from his hand with a fireplace log. As the gun hit the floor, the man in the ski mask swung the log again and hit Peck in the face. Peck partially blocked the log with his arms, but the force of the blow was enough to knock him down.

From the floor, Peck looked up and saw the man in the ski mask take off running. Peck shook off the effects of the blow, picked himself up and gave chase.

By the time Peck reached the first floor, the man in the ski mask was at the door. He ran outside and Peck followed, but the man in the ski mask had already disappeared into the woods by the time Peck reached the fringe of the fire road. He stared into the dark woods, trying to pick up his trail, but it was no use. He could be heading in any direction and if Peck chose the wrong way he could wind up turned around and lost until morning.

Peck returned to the house where he cut the woman loose. She had an immediate breakdown. He did his best to console her as he slipped a robe over her shoulders. Peck poured two stiff drinks from the first-floor bar and gave her one.

"He won't be back," Peck reassured her.

"How do you know?" the woman sobbed between sips of her drink.

"Because you're still alive and I'm a witness."

"But, you'll catch him?" She looked Peck in the eye. "You will catch him, won't you, Sheriff?"

Peck nodded.

"He was going to kill me," the woman said and cried openly again.

"But he didn't and you're still alive and that's what you need to think about," Peck said.

She nodded. "How did you know? That he was here, I mean."

"I didn't," Peck said, thinking fast. "I was patrolling the woods, hoping to run across him. I guess I just got lucky."

The woman nodded again. "It was me that got lucky," she said. Peck studied her face. She was about fifty and attractive. He remembered her from church. She sat close to the front during last Sunday's mass. If nothing else, Peck took some satisfaction in the knowledge that he was right; the killer was using the church to select his victims. How he knew the names and addresses of the victims he selected was another matter. One he would study later when there was more time. If there was more time?

"I'll need my gun," Peck said. He returned to the bedroom and retrieved it from the floor. He also found the kitchen knife the man in the ski mask would have used to cut the woman open.

Entering the living room where the woman sat on the sofa, Peck said, "I have to go if I'm going to pick up his trail."

"You're leaving me?" the woman protested. "What if he comes back?"

"He won't, I told you. And the longer I wait the less chance I have of catching up to him."

The woman began to cry again.

Peck said, "Does your car run?"

The woman sobbed into her hands.

"Your car, does it run?"

The woman raised her face. Dark streaks ran down her cheeks. "Yes."

"Get in it and drive to town and stay at the hospital until we catch him. You'll be safe there."

"Will you wait at least until I get dressed?"

"Yes."

While the woman returned to the bedroom to change, Peck carried the sack of goods he gathered earlier to his snowmobile. When he returned, the woman was ready.

"Drive straight to the hospital," Peck told the woman as she entered her car.

He waited for her to start the engine and drive away on the ice-covered dirt road before he returned to the snowmobile.

It was after midnight by the time Peck returned to the deserted cabin. He ripped off cabinet doors, broke them into pieces, and loaded the wood into the woodstove. He rolled sheets of old yellow newspaper into logs, stuffed them around the wood and used them to ignite a fire.

With a hand-held can opener he took from the woman's house, Peck opened a can of beef stew and baked beans, and set them on the woodstove. He ate a chocolate bar from her kitchen while he waited for the food to heat.

He sat on the bed, lit a cigarette, opened the bottle of bourbon to clear the taste of chocolate from his tongue and mulled things over in his mind. Absolutely nothing made sense. The killer of women and a state trooper ran free while he was the hunted. It was just dumb luck he chose that woman's house to rummage and saved her life. Ten minutes later and he would have stumbled upon victim number four.

Gasoline. He forgot to check the shed for gasoline. There was a quarter of a tank left in the snowmobile. If he were to make a run for the next town, he would need a full tank and maybe extra. He would have to venture out and find a place to fill up.

The stew and beans boiled over and Peck removed them from the woodstove. He ate at the bed and too tired to think anymore, lay down for some much needed sleep.

The dream crept into his sleep as a black cloud in the back of his mind. Slowly, the cloud took shape and color until the form of a young boy appeared. The young boy was on the fireman's ladder, reaching for help as flames raged all around him. The boy's face seemed strangely familiar as he cried loudly for help. The fireman came into view. His out of focus face slowly materialized. The fireman was Peck as a younger man.

In his sleep, Peck gasped and twisted violently on the bed, but didn't wake up.

The dream continued.

He reached for the boy and pulled him to the safety of the ladder. Suddenly from above, burning debris fell from the building and struck the ladder. The boy tried to hold on, but lost his grip. Peck reached for the boy, but the boy fell several flights to his death. Horrified, Peck watched as the boy struck the sidewalk below.

Yelling in his sleep, Peck woke himself with a start and sat up on the bed, gasping for breath. It took several seconds for him to regain his bearings and remember he was alone in the old cabin. He stood up and opened the door for some fresh air to clear his head. The morning sun was warm on his face. The storm had passed and the sky was clear and bright. He lit a cigarette and smoked as he looked at the freshly fallen snow. His tracks were completely covered. He was safe for one more day, but he would have to make his move soon to escape Reese and his men. It struck him then, escape to where? And to do what?

Peck went inside to make a fire. Hardly anything remained of the table. He smashed up the legs, put them into the woodstove, and balled up some of the newspapers. He heated another can of beef stew and ate it on the bed.

As he picked at the stew, Peck glanced at a newspaper on the floor. It was the first time he actually took the time to look at any of them. There was a headline, SOX DEFEAT YANKEES—THE CURSE IS LIFTED.

Peck stared at the headline. The can of beef stew slipped from his hands. Peck reached for the newspaper. It was yellow with age and brittle. He looked at the date of the story. September of 2004.

Peck tossed the newspaper aside and reached for several others. BUSH WINS A SECOND TERM, another headline read. ELECTIONS SUCCESSFUL IN IRAQ, a third quoted.

The newspaper fell to the floor as the room began spinning around inside his head. He tried to steady himself against the wall, but his legs turned to rubber and the room spun around him faster and faster until he slumped to the floor and blacked out.

Peck stirred and slowly awoke on the dusty floor of the cabin. Without his watch, he had no way of knowing how long he lay on the floor, but he judged he had been out for more than an hour by the embers in the woodstove. He stood up cautiously on unsteady legs, picked up the bourbon bottle from the bed and took a good, long drink.

Deb Robertson's house looked cold and uninviting from Peck's vantage point in the woods. It appeared to be unguarded, forgotten. He left the snowmobile in the woods, walked to the garage, and opened the door. There were two five-gallon gas cans on the floor next to her truck.

Peck returned to the snowmobile and drove it into the garage. He refilled the tank, then strapped the second five-gallon can to the back seat with rope his found on a workbench.

He was about to leave when he noticed the connecting door to the house. He tried the door and it was unlocked. Entering the living room, Peck made a quick search by flashlight and found nothing of any use. Reese and his men had done an excellent job of cleanup. He went to the kitchen without any idea of what he was searching for and rummaged the cabinets above and below the sink. There was nothing. If there was, he had overlooked it.

Peck went to the second floor to the master bedroom. The sheets and blankets were missing from the bed. Nothing remained of his encounter with Deb Robertson except the memory of their night together. He opened the walk-in closet and found it empty of all clothing.

Peck turned away, sat on the bed, and lit a cigarette. Reese must have had all of Deb's clothing confiscated for testing, although he couldn't see why. Whatever hair and fiber evidence to be found would come from the bed and rugs, not the clothing in the closet. As he mulled things around in his mind, Peck noticed a piece of tape hanging down from under the top shelf of the closet.

He stood up and walked to the closet, felt under the shelf and ripped the tape away from the wood. A plastic identification card was stuck to the tape. It was unlike any identification card he had ever seen. Deb's photograph was on the left side of the card.

The name under her photograph was Julie A. McNamara. Embossed on the card was the title of a government agency, DEPARTMENT OF DEFENSE.

Peck stared at the card, at Deb's face, trying to make some sense of it all. Then he stuck the card in his shirt pocket and quickly left the house.

The sun was setting behind the tree line as Peck steered the snowmobile over a frozen creek deep within the woods. He had been driving for hours, using the time to think and wait for nightfall. It would be dark in less than fifteen minutes. He drove up a steep hill to a ridge where he parked to smoke a cigarette. Below the ridge, a dirt road was visible. There was a noise and he crouched to watch as a convoy of six Army jeeps passed along the dirt road.

As the last of the jeeps moved from his view, Peck knew he had no place left to turn to for answers. Any information would not be forthcoming, of that he was sure. It was time, he decided, to bring the answers to him.

The wheels were in motion and there was no turning back. As Peck guided the snowmobile deeper into the woods, moonlight failed to penetrate the shrouded cover provided by the thicket of pine trees.

He slowed to a stop near a frozen stream and dismounted. The immediate area looked familiar. He was riding in circles. On your way to get answers, he told himself, you couldn't even find your way out of the forest.

He leaned against the seat of the snowmobile and lit a cigarette. He could reverse direction and follow his own tracks back to the ridge where he spotted the jeeps. If he followed the road the jeeps traveled on, he . . .

Peck heard the sudden noise of another snowmobile. It was close. The sound came from due west of where he sat. He listened closely and the sound appeared to be heading away from him.

Peck bolted off the snowmobile and turned to face the direction of the noise. The Army or National Guard or whatever the hell they were would not send one man to look for him. Either it was another resident out for a joyride and at the price of a snowmobile, not many in town could afford one, or the man in the ski mask.

Peck mounted the snowmobile, started the engine and took off due west. He raced for one mile, then slowed to a stop and shut the engine off. The other snowmobile echoed in the distance. From the sound of its engine, it was traveling at maximum speed.

Peck started the engine and continued on his course. Another mile and he came to an unmarked dirt road. He shut the engine down to listen. There was only silence. Either the other snowmobile had changed direction and its sound was heading away from him, or it had shut down and parked.

Peck started his engine and slowly glided across the dirt road. When he reached the other side, Peck steered the snowmobile to the left and used its powerful headlight to check for houses. There were none and he reversed direction. Straining his eyesight, Peck could make out the faint outline of a home about a thousand yards up the road.

Peck gunned the engine and raced toward the home. As he neared it, he could see the home was a one-story, Tudor-style building. Light was not visible from anywhere inside the home. Its chimney appeared cold and uninviting.

Peck slowed the snowmobile to a crawl. Maybe he was mistaken in his assumption the stalker was out prowling. He could be chasing some kid who borrowed dad's machine for a midnight joyride.

As Peck slowly approached the Tudor-style home, he passed a massive oak tree and the man in the ski mask leapt from behind it and swung a large tree branch at Peck. Throwing his arms up, Peck took the brunt of the hit on his forearms.

Peck fell from the snowmobile to the hard snow. The snowmobile skidded out and struck the oak tree, barely missing his attacker. As Peck shook off the effects of the fall, the man in the ski mask ran toward his snowmobile parked behind the oak tree.

Peck jumped up, raced toward his attacker, and reached him just as he was pulling a rifle from a side holster on the snowmobile. Peck hit the man high and together they spilled over the snowmobile, crashed to the snow on the other side, and broke apart.

The man in the ski mask jumped up first and reached for the rifle that had fallen several feet away from them. Peck rolled over, jumped and hit the man on the legs. The man kicked Peck in the face with a heavy boot and shook Peck loose. The man in the ski mask grabbed the rifle by its stock. Peck reached for his revolver, but it lay ten feet away in the snow. Having no choice, Peck charged the man in the ski mask again and took him down by the legs. They rolled, kicking and punching each other until they hit the base of the oak tree and came to an abrupt stop.

Peck got up first and as the man in the ski mask rose up, Peck punched him in the stomach and he doubled over. Peck hit him with a right uppercut to straighten him out, then clubbed him with several unanswered blows to the face.

The man in the ski mask hit the oak tree and slowly slumped to the ground. Peck was about to reach for the mask when the sudden noise of Army jeeps on the road froze him in his tracks. Headlights were suddenly upon him, blinding him.

Someone shouted, “There. I see him.”

Peck looked around for his revolver, picked it up and ran to his snowmobile. As he raced away into the woods, shots rang out. There was no way to tell if the shots were meant for him or the man in the ski mask, not without turning around and he was not about to do that.

“Don’t you move,” someone else shouted, and Peck assumed the order was aimed at the man in the ski mask. Again, Peck was not about to turn around to find out.

Ten

Reese, six of his men, McCoy and Kranston occupied the main hall of the logging camp. Kranston's face and demeanor showed his disapproval at the present set of circumstances. He chewed several sticks of gum at once, which meant his annoyance level was at an all-time high.

A fire crackled in the stone fireplace while a generator hummed in the background and provided power for the lights. For many long seconds, the only sound in the room was the fire crackling and Kranston's gum chewing.

Then the door opened and two of Reese's men escorted Linda Boyce into the hall. She could barely walk and they shouldered most of her weight as they helped her sit on the sofa.

Kranston inspected her face and eyes, rolling back her eyelids. If aware of what was happening to her, Linda didn't protest. "She's a fucking basket case. Tom, I thought you said she . . ."

"She isn't that bad, Ed," McCoy commented. "We can bring her around."

"Bring her around? From what, comatose to unconscious?" Kranston glared at McCoy, and then shifted his attention to Reese. "An army of men and you've lost him."

"We haven't lost him, Ed," Reese said. "We just haven't found him yet."

"Explain to me the difference so maybe I can understand that idiotic line of reasoning," Kranston snapped.

"We're doing all . . ."

"Shut up," Kranston scolded Reese. "My give a damn is broken when it comes to your excuses. I expect more from the world's largest intelligence agency than failure and bullshit excuses for failure."

Reese held his tongue and glared at Kranston.

"What, nothing to say?" Kranston said.

"I have eighteen two-man teams out right now looking for him. It's a big town, Ed." Reese said.

"It's a big town, Ed," Kranston said, mocking Reese. "And the last time I looked, there was a big fence around it."

"Ed, what do we do about her?" McCoy said and pointed a finger at Linda.

Kranston stood over Linda and checked her eyes. "She's too far gone to do anything with her here. We need to relocate her to the lab. Maybe we can save her there."

McCoy nodded. "We'll do it in the morning."

Kranston nodded to McCoy, and then looked at Reese. "And I'll expect Peck in custody by morning. Is that clear?"

"Yes," Reese said, subserviently.

"Otherwise, don't bother coming back," Kranston said. He turned and walked toward the front door. "Doctor McCoy and I will be in my private lab. Call us there the moment you have found Peck. And if I hear of anymore shooting, somebody's ass will be on my trophy wall. Understood?"

Silently, Reese nodded to Kranston.

Kranston and McCoy exited the main hall and walked toward Kranston's late-model Ford sedan. As Kranston reached for the car door handle, Peck emerged from the shadows and struck him across the bridge of the nose with his revolver. As Kranston fell to the snow, Peck quickly aimed the revolver at McCoy.

"Move, Tom," Peck said. "Do it."

McCoy backed away from the car and raised his hands. He glanced down at Kranston and saw a pool of blood in the snow.

Kranston moaned as he worked his way to his knees. Blood poured from his nose into his mouth and he spit out his gum. Peck looked at him. "Nice to see you again, Ed. We have some catching up to do."

Peck looked at McCoy. "Help him up."

McCoy came around the other side of the Ford and lifted Kranston to his feet. Kranston wiped blood on the sleeve of his jacket.

"Dave . . . we've been looking for you," Kranston said.

"Really," Peck said. "Mind telling me what for?"

"He's hurt, Dave," McCoy said. "We need to get him inside."

"Where Reese and his men are waiting for me," Peck said.

"No need to go inside for that, we're right here," Reese said from behind Peck.

Peck turned around. Reese and his six men were on the front steps of the main hall. They held rifles at the ready. Reese aimed a semiautomatic pistol at Peck.

"The guns aren't necessary," Kranston said.

Peck grabbed Kranston from behind and shoved the barrel of his revolver against Kranston's throat. "Yes they are," Peck said.

"Lower your weapons," Kranston ordered Reese.

"So he can blow your head off," Reese said.

"You idiot, he isn't worth spit to us unless he's alive," Kranston said.

Peck pressed the revolver into Kranston's flesh. "I'd do as he says, Reese. I have been somewhat jumpy these days. The gun might go off by accident. Boom, it's a mess."

Reese and Peck entered into a stare-down. Finally, Reese lowered his pistol and nodded to his men. They lowered their rifles.

"Toss them in the snow," Peck said.

Reese tossed his pistol. His men threw the rifles into a snowdrift aside the porch.

"Handguns, too," Peck said. "And that backup weapon you keep on your ankle, Reese. I spotted that the first day."

They did as ordered and Peck lowered his revolver to the square of Kranston's back. "So, Ed," Peck said. "What am I worth dead?"

"Nothing," Kranston said.

"What's that mean, Ed? Huh?" Peck shoved hard against Kranston's back and he nearly fell over.

McCoy said, "It means you cost the US government one billion dollars, you goddamn idiot."

Peck spun Kranston around and looked him in the eye. "What the hell is he talking about, Ed? What?"

"It's very uncomfortable out here in the cold, Dave," Kranston said.

"You want uncomfortable, I'll pull the trigger," Peck said.

"Okay, but can we talk inside? I'm freezing."

Peck looked at Reese. "Get inside with your backs against the wall. Do it."

Reese looked at Kranston who nodded.

"Don't look at him, I'm the one with the gun," Peck said.

"Smart move, giving him real bullets," Reese said.

"How long do you think it would have taken him to figure out he had blanks?" Kranston said.

Reese glared at Peck as he turned and led his men inside the hall where they stood with their backs against the far wall opposite the front door.

"Now you," Peck said to McCoy.

McCoy entered the hall and stood next to Reese.

"Our turn," Peck said and dug the revolver into Kranston's back. They entered the hall and Peck shoved Kranston onto the sofa. Peck stepped back and looked around the hall. "There, we're all together again. Just like a staff meeting. Should we discuss next year's budget? I could use a new deputy. My current one is broken."

"So is my nose," Kranston said.

"I don't care," Peck said.

"Well I do," McCoy said.

Peck looked at McCoy. "Move and I'll shoot you, Tom. Or is that your name?"

Kranston said, "David, I need to ask . . ."

"I'll ask the questions," Peck said.

"So ask one."

With his left hand, Peck removed the identification card he found at Deb Robertson's house. He held it up to Kranston. "Why is Deb Robertson, Julie McNamara? Can you explain that to me, Ed?"

Kranston looked at the identification card. "Julie McNamara is, or was her real name," he said. "Deb Robertson was an alias."

"Why did she need a fake name, Ed?" Peck said.

"It's . . . complicated." Kranston dug out his gum and placed a stick into his mouth.

"Simplify it."

"That isn't as easy as it sounds."

"Simplify it even more."

Reese suddenly moved off the wall. "For Christ's sake, Ed. How much more of this bullshit are we going to take?"

"Shut up," Kranston said, turning to look at Reese.

Peck looked at Reese. "Yeah, shut up."

"When this is over," Reese said.

Peck smacked Kranston across the bridge of his already broken nose. Kranston doubled over and nearly fell from the sofa.

"What the fuck did you do that for?" McCoy said.

"Every time he misbehaves," Peck said, and nodded to Reese,

"Ed gets another one."

"He's bleeding like a stuck pig, for God's sake," McCoy said. "You want answers, but he can't give them to you if he's unconscious."

"Fix him up," Peck said. He looked at Reese. "Anybody else moves, he won't move again."

McCoy rushed to Kranston's side and sat him up on the sofa. "Jesus Christ, Dave. Is this necessary?" McCoy said.

Peck looked at Reese. "Tell him to behave and it won't be."

"I need a towel and water," McCoy said.

Peck nodded to Reese with the revolver. "Get it and only it."

Reese moved to an ice-filled cooler against the wall, removed a bottle of water, and brought it to McCoy.

"There's a towel in the bathroom. Okay if I get it?" Reese said.

"No." Peck aimed the revolver at McCoy. "You get it."

McCoy backed away to the bathroom where he found a towel on a rack.

Peck looked at Reese. "Your feet stuck?"

Reese stepped backward and returned to the wall. McCoy brought the towel to the sofa, poured water on it and wiped blood from Kranston's face.

"He's going to need stitches," McCoy said.

"Later," Peck said. "Now Ed, explain to me how a homicide investigation turns into the CIA hunting the sheriff?"

"Not hunting, looking for," Kranston said.

"Explain to me the difference." Peck looked past McCoy at a coffee pot that rested on the woodstove. "Is it hot?"

McCoy shrugged and looked at Reese.

"Yes," Reese said.

Peck motioned to McCoy. "Pour me a cup."

McCoy picked up a mug from the table, walked to the woodstove to fill it with coffee and brought it to Peck. "Back to the wall, Tom," Peck said.

McCoy returned to his spot next to Reese.

Peck took a sip from the mug and sighed with great satisfaction at the taste of the hot coffee. "Now Ed, when I was hiding from the men who aren't chasing me, I came across an old cabin in the woods. It's been abandoned for a long time. Do you know what I found there?"

"No."

"Something very interesting," Peck said. "bunch of old newspapers. Most were yellow with age and fell apart when I picked them up. I used them to start a fire until one caught my eye. Know what it said?"

"Newspapers, for God's sake. Is there a point to this?" Reese demanded.

"You know, Reese, Ed's face can't take much more abuse," Peck said.

"Reese, will you just shut the fuck up," McCoy shouted to Reese.

"We all seem to be a bit jumpy," Peck said and set the coffee mug aside and used his left hand to reach into a jacket pocket for a folded sheet of newspaper. He tossed it to Kranston. "Read it."

Kranston unfolded the paper and scanned the headline.

"What does it say?" Peck said.

"Bush wins a second term," Kranston said.

"What month?"

"November."

"What year?"

"2004."

Peck picked up the mug and took a sip. "Now I ask you, Ed. How is it possible for this Bush to win an election forty-five years from now? Answer me that, Ed. Huh?"

Against the wall, Reese suddenly moved his left leg.

"Nobody said you could move," Peck said.

"I have a cramp," Reese explained.

"Move again, you'll have a bullet."

"Do as he says," Kranston said. "I have everything under control."

"You do, huh?" Peck said. "Then how about you give me some answers."

"It will take a while," Kranston said. "Why don't you sit down? Keep the gun if you like."

"I wasn't planning on giving it up."

"At least get comfortable."

"Quit stalling," Peck shouted. He waved the revolver in Kranston's face.

"All right, Dave, all right," Kranston said. "Just stay calm. Please."

Peck pulled out his cigarettes and lit one, looking at Kranston. "I'm calm and I'm listening. Start talking."

"My name really is Edward Kranston. I work for the Department of Defense."

"The Defense Department?"

"Yes."

"And what do you do for the Department of Defense, Ed?"

"I'm a psychiatrist."

"You mean a shrink?"

"I specialize in schizophrenia. Know what that is?"

"I've heard of it."

"It's a disorder where the victim has multiple personalities."

"You mean crazy," Peck said. "Am I crazy, Ed? Is that what you're saying?"

"No, you're not crazy, Dave," Kranston said. "However, you are seriously damaged."

"What's that mean, seriously damaged?"

Kranston used the wet towel to wipe blood, which began to

drip from his nose again. "In private practice, I attracted the attention of the government when I was able to completely cure the personality of a schizophrenia patient."

"None of that bullshit explains any of this," Peck said.

"No, it doesn't."

Reese moved his left leg again and Peck turned and shot him in the knee. Everybody inside the room except Peck jumped. The sound of the gunshot, amplified inside the cabin was near deafening. Screaming, Reese fell to the floor and held his bloody left kneecap.

"You shot him," Kranston said.

"He moved," Peck said.

"If I move, will you shoot me, too?" McCoy said.

Peck shook his head and McCoy knelt to Reese. "Oh this is just great," McCoy said. "I'll need to carry him . . ."

"No," Peck shouted. "He stays where he is. Stop the bleeding, but he stays on the floor." Peck looked at Kranston. "You were saying?"

Unshaken by the shooting, Kranston set the bloody towel aside. "I was asked by the government . . . no, make that recruited by the government to work on a secret program they were developing. Are you familiar with the term mind control, Dave?"

"Brainwashing," Peck said.

"It's far more complicated than that, I'm afraid." Kranston's tone seemed to gain strength as he spoke. "The Chinese first experimented with it after the Korean War."

"Chinese? What the fuck are you talking about, the Chinese? What does any of that have to do with me or Deb or whatever the hell her name is?" Peck said.

"All of it," Kranston said.

Still kneeling over Reese, McCoy looked at Peck. "The bullet needs to come out."

Peck smiled at Kranston. "My give a damn is broken," he said, repeating Kranston's phrase.

"He'll bleed to death," McCoy insisted.

"Take it out then, just don't move him off the floor," Peck said.

"There's an extra sofa," Kranston said. "What harm would it do to move him?"

"I can't watch three places with only two eyes," Peck said. "Now go on with with your story."

Kranston sighed to himself. "The wars never seem to end. Korea, Vietnam, Iraq, Iran and back to Korea again. After the Muslim uprising in Russia, the world community knew we were on the path to global annihilation as a race. Something had to be done before half the world nuked the other half."

"You're talking, but you're not saying anything that explains anything to do with what's going on around here, Ed," Peck said. "You're a true politician."

"We develop bigger and better weapons, but we can't exactly nuke the entire world," Kranston said. "Don't you agree?"

"Agree?" Peck laughed softly to himself. "I have no idea what the hell you're talking about."

"I'm talking about final and everlasting peace, Dave. No more Vietnams, Iraqs or Russian incidents to worry about. Millions and millions of people who died for their causes would now live for them instead."

Suddenly sweating, Peck wiped his face on his shirtsleeve. "There have been no such wars. Except for Korea, I've heard of no such wars."

"Imagine for a moment the possibility of taking a brutal dictator and giving him a personality makeover," Kranston said. "He does a one-eighty and we don't have to invade his shitty little sandbox of a country to free a population which hates us anyway and doesn't want us there to begin with. A lot of American boys are spared and everybody is happy on the home front."

With his left hand, Peck reached for a spot between his eyes and rubbed it.

"Peace would be ensured without a shot being fired," Kranston said. "America becomes a true peacekeeper and the idea of democracy finally is an obtainable goal."

"Even if I knew what you were babbling about, none of that is possible," Peck said. The pressure between his eyes grew slightly.

"But it is possible, Dave," Kranston said. "And completely within our grasp."

Peck had to squint through the sweat running down his forehead to look at Kranston.

"Combine the right drugs with the correct methods and create the ultimate weapon of mass destruction, a makeover for the human mind," Kranston said.

"What does any of that have to do with me?" Peck said. "Or Bender and Reese and the others?"

"You are part of a five-year plan, David," Kranston explained. "And part of a great experiment which could end all the hatred and lead to global peace. However, you were a broken man in need of a great deal of fixing."

Peck's breathing grew labored as the pain between his eyes intensified.

"The government gave me unlimited funding to build this secret military base and stock it with men and women of my choosing."

"Military base?"

"Yes. That's what this entire town and surrounding land is, Dave," Kranston said. "One, big military base. Top secret, of course."

"That's why the fence?"

"Yes."

"And the Army running around?"

"Yes."

"You said." Peck paused to wipe sweat from his face and massage his forehead. "Stock it with men and women like Noah's fucking ark. What men, what women?"

"Those who suffered breakdowns," Kranston said. "Some mild, some complete. They came from all lifestyles and occupations. Like yourself."

The revolver in Peck's hand felt heavy and he lowered it to his side. He squinted through the sweat and pain at Kranston. "Myself?"

"A shut in, a woman who hadn't spoken a word in ten years. A serial killer who . . ."

"Serial killer? You know who murdered Deb and the others?"

"Sadly, yes," Kranston admitted.

"And you allowed it to happen?"

"Not allowed, David. Observed. It's all part of the greater plan."

"You're fucking insane," Peck said.

"Am I?" Kranston said. "Two hundred of the three hundred people on this base are patients. I gave them a new life and a new personality, but you are the prize, David. I didn't plan on the storm or the man responsible for the murders regressing, but once it happened, it was the perfect opportunity to see how well you performed under maximum stress."

Peck backed up as the revolver fell to the floor. "Shut up," Peck screamed. "Just shut up."

"I chose January for the isolation and set the wheels in motion," Kranston said. "I made it appear 1959 for the simplicity and ease of that era. The night of the ice storm was your first night out of the lab." Kranston's voice quivered with excitement as he spoke and his eyes seemed to come alive. "From that moment when you opened your eyes in what you believed was your bed, all that you knew and remembered is what I put there. The way you slipped into your new life with such ease proves my theory and research to be the way to finally win the peace the world deserves. It's a great day in history, David."

"Bullshit. This place is nothing but a giant lab for you to test your rats in," Peck said.

"That's a simple, but accurate description."

Peck gasped for air as his chest suddenly felt heavy. The pain in his head spread to his skull and it was difficult to see and focus.

"Who was . . . Deb . . . I mean Julie?"

"A research scientist attached to the project. She volunteered to test you under . . . sexual pressure. That was my idea. An experiment to see your reaction with the added burden of female . . . company."

"Sexual . . . and you let her die? Was that part of your great plan, too?"

"It was an unfortunate incident," Kranston said. "It was unforeseen and tragic."

"And me? Who am I?" Peck sobbed.

"You know who you are, David," Kranston said. "It's locked deep within you, but it's still there." Kranston paused to tap his skull with a finger. "Do you want to let it out?"

"Yes."

"It will be painful."

Peck felt weak in the knees and slowly slumped to the floor. "Painful? You should see what's inside my head right now."

"I know what's in your head, David. I put it there. All those memories and feelings of your past are nothing more than what I programmed you to believe was real. They are not. The real life you knew is locked away deep inside you. Buried."

From his knees, Peck looked at Kranston.

"Want to see it?" Kranston said.

Peck nodded his head. "Yes."

"Your real name is John David Peck and ten years ago you suffered a complete mental breakdown after the death of your son," Kranston said. "If you allow them to reemerge, the memories will come."

Peck sat on his heels and closed his eyes. He felt hot, as if his brain were on fire. In the darkness behind his eyes, something struggled to get out. That something terrified him. He pitched forward and caught himself of the palms of his hands and then that something began to emerge in the form of memory.

Captain David Peck was in his office at the fire station when the five-alarm call rang out. He dropped the labor reports he was working on and rushed to his gear. Even with all of today's modern equipment and technology, there was nothing to compare to the rush he felt at the sound of the bell.

Peck rode in his car ahead of the trucks. His lieutenant, a man named Brooks, drove. Peck studied the global positioning unit mounted on the dashboard.

"It's that abandoned tenement building on the fourteen hundred block, near your neighborhood," Brooks said.

Peck knew the building. Scheduled for demolition next month, maybe the fire would do the job instead. From his laptop, Peck ran a check on the fifty-year-old building. Erected during the late sixties, it was a wood and brick structure, built without the fire retardant materials and wiring of today. It would burn long, hot, and barbecue everything in its interior.

Brooks glanced at Peck. "There's a report kids were playing in the building."

Peck felt an immediate panic in his chest. He had told his eleven-year-old son to stay out of that building a hundred times, but he and his friends always snuck back to play in the abandoned halls and search for discarded treasure.

Peck looked at Brooks. "Are we going the whole way in second gear? Step on it."

"The fire was quite an event, the biggest one of the year," Kranston said. "When I found you, I did a records search and created a scrapbook for research purposes. What a mess you were."

Ahead of the hook and ladder trucks, Peck and Brooks arrived at the burning tenement building.

Peck exited the car and looked up at the building. It was beyond saving. A crowd had gathered to watch the fire and Peck recognized several boys in the crowd as friends of his son.

"James is still up there," a boy shouted to Peck.

"I can't imagine what that must have felt like at that exact moment," Kranston said. "The pain you must have felt had to be pure agony."

Peck raised his head and looked at Kranston. Tears rolled down Peck's cheeks as the memory of that day became clearer in his mind.

Dressed in full gear, Peck began to climb the ladder on a truck. Brooks attempted to pull him off.

"Get away from me," Peck shouted. "My son is up there."

"It's too dangerous," Brooks said, but it was no use.

Peck climbed the ladder to the fourth floor of the tenement building where his eleven-year-old son, James, hung out the window and cried for help.

"Dad," James shouted.

"Give me your hand," Peck cried. He reached as far as the ladder would allow and the boy was able to take hold and jump to the first rung. The ladder swayed, but held fast.

"Down. Take us down," Peck shouted to his men below.

The ladder slowly moved away from the building. James began to descend along the rungs when a large hunk of burning debris suddenly broke loose from the building, struck the ladder, and shook it violently.

"Hold on, James. Hold on," Peck shouted as he slipped several rungs before regaining his grip.

"Dad," James cried.

Peck climbed as quickly as he could, but the boy lost his grip before he reached him. Stunned and horrified, Peck could only helplessly watch as his only son fell several stories to his death below.

On his knees, the memory of the event intact and clear, Peck wept openly.

"Well, you could imagine what kind of impact that would have on a father," Kranston said. "Any father. However, a firefighter losing his only son at a fire, that is enough to put anyone over the edge. You came to my attention a year later when I was researching possible subjects. You were little more than a living vegetable."

Peck raised his head. "So you resurrected me to be your lab rat? You sick son of a bitch, you're insane."

"Am I? I am not the one walking around with someone else's mind, David. Even the questions Reese and the others asked you during the course of the murder investigation were written by me. I control it all and for what it's worth, you did very well the first time out of the box."

Peck forced his way to his feet. His brain was on fire. He stared at Kranston until his vision cleared. "People died, you sick, twisted fuck."

"David, a few people died," Kranston said, nonchalantly. "Isn't that worth it to save millions? Knowing that a few, faceless mentally ill people would die to accomplish that task, wouldn't you have to do it? Wouldn't you have to think of the greater good, even if a few, insignificant lives are lost?"

"Who . . . am I?" Peck said. "Goddamn you, who am I?"

"You are whoever I program you to be," Kranston said.

"What year is this?"

Kranston smiled at Peck. "2019. Welcome to the future, Dave."

Peck rubbed his eyes and looked at Kranston. His vision was a blur. "I had a wife. I remember now. That night at Deb's, I could feel her, but I couldn't see her face. She was blond and pretty. What was her name?"

"Oh, I don't think you want to know."

Peck took a step toward Kranston, then paused as his eyes rolled back exposing the whites. Slowly, Peck sunk to the floor where he passed out.

McCoy rushed forward and knelt beside Peck. He pulled back Peck's right eyelid to inspect his eye. "He's completely regressed, Ed."

"But savable," Kranston said. "If we hurry."

McCoy turned and motioned to Reese's men. "Help me get him to the main lab. Get the girl, too."

"What about me?" Reese said. "I'm shot here. I'm bleeding all over myself."

"I'll fix you up in no time. Don't worry," McCoy said.

As Reese's men lifted Peck and carried him out, Peck's cigarettes fell from his pocket. Kranston picked the cigarette pack up and sat on the sofa.

At the door, McCoy turned to look at Kranston. "Ed, are you coming?"

"I'll be along," Kranston said, removing his gum.

Several of his men carried Reese out to a waiting car. Kranston was alone. He removed one of Peck's cigarettes and lit it with a match. It had been so long since he smoked, but damn it all, they were still so good.

ELEVEN

Peck hummed to himself as he shaved before his bathroom mirror using a sleek and efficient electric razor, the newest model available, the one with five floating heads and guide bar. After shaving, he felt the smoothness of his skin, splashed on some aftershave, and then inspected his face carefully. While slight bags had settled recently under his eyes, his overall appearance was not that of your average fifty-four-year-old man. His hair was thick and dark, his chin void of the normal middle age sag. The muscles in his arms and shoulders bulged with the strength of his youth and his chest and stomach were firm and flat.

Pleased with his appearance, he left the bathroom and wandered into the large, ultramodern, gleaming white kitchen. Filling a stainless steel coffee pot with purified tap water, Peck set it on the latest coffee maker from France to brew. While he waited, he used a dishtowel to wipe down the ceramic countertop tiles until they shined.

When the coffee was ready, Peck filled a mug, reached for his cigarettes on the table and walked to the window. He lit a cigarette and looked through the spotless glass. Trees were beginning to bud, as were flowers. The sun was high and warm and he was growing anxious to go outside, walk around and smell the spring air after being cooped up like a house cat for months.

From his office in the main lab, Ed Kranston made notes in a book as he sat on a sofa and watched Peck on one of a dozen monitors. As Peck moved from room to room, a different camera picked him up and showed Kranston exactly what he was doing at every moment. Audio recorded every word Peck spoke, to himself and others. Even the phone had a direct feed to Kranston's equipment so he could monitor Peck's social progress.

Behind Kranston, the office door opened and Tom McCoy entered. "How is he doing today?" McCoy said, joining Kranston of the sofa.

"He looks terrific," Kranston said. "But a bit antsy."

"Spring fever." McCoy looked at a monitor and watched Peck smoke a cigarette by the kitchen window. "He's come a long way in four months."

"Yes."

"You don't sound happy."

Kranston looked at McCoy. "It's that meeting with Justice."

"What about it?"

"They want the timeline moved up."

"That's impossible. They know that."

Kranston shook his head. "We know that. They don't know anything."

"Then we'll have to make them understand that work like this takes years of planning and development before it's perfected," McCoy said. "This isn't the fast food industry here."

"That's the problem," Kranston sighed. "They know it takes years, but they want it in months."

"Months?" McCoy said. "It can't be done in months."

Kranston watched Peck move from the kitchen to the living room where he sat on the sofa and clicked on the sixty-inch television. "You've heard about the latest uprising in the Middle East?"

"Who hasn't. It's been all over the news since last week. Just when we thought peace would last among the tribes, a new nutcase arrives on the scene and starts cutting heads off again."

"Nutcase or not, remember what happened the last time we ignored a state of affairs like that. It blew up in everyone's face. Two million were dead before the UN called its first meeting. It will be worse this time. A lot worse."

McCoy sighed as he watched Peck light a cigarette on the monitor.

"They want the CIA to go in and begin infiltration as soon as possible," Kranston said. "The quicker they can turn his high ranking staff against this new would-be dictator the faster we quell the violence."

"What did you tell them?"

"I told them I would present the results at the meeting and let them decide what to do from there."

"By results, you mean Peck?"

"Yes."

McCoy looked at Peck on the monitor. He was motionless on the sofa, seemingly uninterested in the television. "What's he doing?"

"Waiting," Kranston said.

"For what?"

"Me."

Peck's head was hurting again. Not the overpowering pressure and pain as he experienced in the past, but just enough to encourage him to lie down.

He stared at the pure white ceiling in his bedroom as he waited for the pain to subside. He didn't remember painting it white, but he must have. After all, this was his house.

The same argument could be made of the bedroom furniture. It was the latest in fashion and design, sleek and efficient, unisex in nature. He didn't remember buying it, but he must have. It was here. So was everything else.

The pressure behind his eyes finally dissipated enough for him to stand up. He went to the bathroom where he washed his face with stinging cold water. The freezing effect always made him feel better around the eyes.

He wondered if he should take the medication Ed gave him for the pain. He decided against it. There was no sense in wasting a pill if the pain had left on its own.

Peck went to the first floor of his house and entered the living room where he turned on the television. There was never anything interesting to watch. Using a remote, he flipped channels until he settled on a cable news program. There was unrest in the Middle East, protests in Russia, demonstrators in Washington, atrocities in Africa. What else was new?

Peck glanced at the heavy watch around his left wrist. It was nearly four in the afternoon. A slight case of anticipation was bubbling inside his stomach. He lit a cigarette and smoked it to the filter.

The front doorbell rang and Peck jumped up from the sofa. That would be Ed.

Kranston sat in a chair opposite the sofa and carefully inspected Peck, who occupied the seat opposite him on the sofa. A briefcase rested on Kranston's lap.

"How are you today, Dave?"

"I'm fine Ed, how are you?"

"Good."

"Did you bring my cigarettes?"

Kranston opened the briefcase, removed a carton of cigarettes, and rested it on the coffee table. "Have I ever forgotten?"

Peck picked up the carton and removed a pack. "Would you like some coffee, Ed? I just made it."

"Yes, I would."

They moved to the kitchen where they sat at the table while

Peck poured coffee into two mugs.

Peck lit a cigarette. "I want to go outside, Ed."

"Soon."

"When?"

"As soon as the doctors say you're fit to resume your duties as police chief."

Peck took a sip of coffee. "I feel fine. I want to walk around and smell the fresh air."

"I think what they're worried about is your mental condition, Dave." Kranston looked at Peck as he sipped coffee. "After all, when a man has been in a car accident like the one which put you into a coma like that, they err on the side of caution. It's for your own benefit."

"But I feel fine. My mind is as clear as a bell and I hardly have headaches anymore."

"I hope so, Dave. The doctors want to test you next week."

"Test me? How?"

"I'm not sure. With questions, I would imagine."

"What kind of questions?"

Kranston shrugged his shoulders. "Questions to determine your state of mind, as I understand it."

"Maybe I should get ready, then," Peck suggested.

"Good idea. I can help."

"How?"

"I can test you. For instance, who is the president of Russia?"

Seated on the sofa in Kranston's office, McCoy watched and listened with keen interest as Kranston asked one question after another to Peck. To Peck's credit, he got nearly every one right.

Pleased with Peck's progress, McCoy stood up and walked to the window to look out. Peck wasn't the only one experiencing spring fever. It was a long, hard winter, spent mostly indoors at the secret lab where the artificial lighting wreaked havoc with your eyes after several months of intense exposure to it.

Outside the window, grass showed the first signs of growing, as did flowers and trees. In the background, McCoy heard Kranston continue questioning Peck.

A quote he read once in college by Publilius Syrus in 42 B.C., flashed through his mind. "It is sometimes expedient to forget who we are," Syrus said. Never was that quote more appropriate.

Twelve

The state of Maine was experiencing its worst heat wave in a decade during the week of the Fourth of July. Temperatures reached one hundred and one degrees by noon of the third. As Peck drove his sleek, ultramodern police cruiser through the center of Dunston Falls, he was grateful for its powerful air-conditioning unit. Earlier models of the hybrid police vehicles didn't have the power of the old gas-guzzlers and the AC was always weak.

Peck parked in his reserved spot outside the four-story municipal building, next to the town mayor's car. Exiting the cruiser, Peck climbed the steps of the municipal building where he paused to look at the banner that stretched across Main Street. HAPPY FOURTH OF JULY 2019, DUNSTON FALLS, the banner read.

Peck entered the modern municipal building, which housed the six-man police force he was head of, the mayor's office, tax assessor, code enforcement officer, the DOT and school board. Only the police department and small holding cells occupied the first floor.

As Peck entered his office, his senior man, Lieutenant Reese, greeted him from his desk against the wall. "Morning, Chief. The mayor is in your office."

"Ed? What does he want?" Peck said.

"Don't know. He wouldn't say."

Peck picked up a coffee mug and filled it from the double

burner, French-made coffee machine. "I guess I'll go see."

Peck's private office was located at the rear of the large central office and enclosed behind a large window and glass door. The words Captain David Peck were stenciled on the glass door in white lettering.

"Good morning, Dave," Kranston said when Peck entered his office.

"Ed," Peck nodded. "What can I do for you?"

"Close the door."

Peck closed the door and took a seat behind his desk. Kranston occupied the chair facing the desk.

"Dave," Kranston began. "We have almost sixteen thousand residents in our town. Another ten thousand are expected for tomorrow's celebration."

Peck took a sip of his coffee. "You don't want a repeat of last year."

"That's right," Kranston said. "But, you've only been here ten months, how do you know about last year?"

"I can read reports, Ed."

"Yes, of course."

"Relax, Ed. I didn't work twenty-five years in New York City and not learn a few things about crowd control."

"I realize that," Kranston said, removing the wrapper from a stick of gum. "I guess I'm just jumpy. These celebrations are very important to the economy of small towns. Maybe you could give me an overview for tomorrow night." Kranston placed the stick of gum into his mouth and looked at Peck.

Peck sipped coffee, and then picked up a folder from his desk. He flipped it open to the first page. "The fair begins at five p.m. I will have my entire staff posted on the ground from start to finish, beginning at three. I will be there as well. There are six reserve officers for backup duty and they will be on walking patrol. The fire department will have an EMT truck posted at entrances, north and south. Doctor McCoy and several nurses from the hospital will be on duty at aid stations around the park. The fireworks will begin at nine and will run forty-five minutes. The fire chief has coordinated the event with the pyrotechnics team hired by the town council." Peck paused to look at Kranston. "Of which you are head of."

"What about the underage drinking?" Kranston said. "That was the main concern of the council after last year's disaster. Another incident like that and the council will vote to shut down the fair."

"All vendors are on alert," Peck reassured Kranston. "If any of them are caught selling alcohol to kids, they will be arrested on the spot and banned from future events."

Kranston looked at Peck. "It sounds like you've covered all the bases."

"There's always a last-minute detail, but I'm confident tomorrow will go off without a hitch."

"Well," Kranston said and stood up. "I'll be in my office. Let me know if there is anything you need."

Kranston left Peck's office and walked through the main office to the door. As he passed Reese, they made brief eye contact. Kranston appeared to give Reese a tiny nod.

Around twelve-thirty, Peck set aside his paperwork and walked to the main office. Only Reese, recovering from a line-of-duty gunshot wound, was around.

"Feel like lunch?" Peck said. "I'll buy."

"What if there's a 911 call?" Reese said.

"Put the phones on call forward to my cell phone," Peck said. "We can always relay it to a car in the field."

"Just like in the big cities." Reese stood up from his desk and walked to the door with a noticeable limp in his left leg.

Peck and Reese crossed Main Street and entered Deb's

Diner. The sleek, ultramodern restaurant combined new age and art deco architecture in its décor. Peck and Reese found a booth near the window. The diner hummed with activity.

A short, blond woman of about thirty approached Peck and Reese. She held a coffeepot and smiled at them. "Coffee?"

Peck and Reese turned their cups over and she filled them.

"What are the specials today, Deb?" Reese asked.

"The meatloaf is heaven," Deb said. "I made it myself."

Peck and Reese looked at each other. "Two," Peck said.

Deb smiled and went to get their orders.

Peck said, "How is the leg today?" looking at Reese.

"Stiff. It's been a year, but I still can't believe that kid shot me over a speeding ticket," Reese said. "I think Doctor McCoy is taking the brace off the knee next week. God knows, I'm ready."

Peck looked at Reese. "He's a good man, Doctor McCoy."

"Yes," Reese said. "He is."

Peck drove to his large, two-story home on the west side of town. Situated off a back road in the woods, it faced a small pond. His nearest neighbor was a thousand yards to the right.

Having grown up and lived most of his life in a city of nine million, the quiet, country setting was a welcome change of pace, even if it took some getting used to at first.

Peck removed the heavy utility belt around his waist and set it on a coat hook in the foyer. He went to the kitchen for a can of beer, opened the sliding doors and stepped out to the backyard. The lawn needed mowing. He sat in a patio chair, lit a cigarette and listened to the slight breeze waft through the tall pine trees. He looked up and the tips of the trees rocked gently as the breeze continued to blow. The temperature had fallen to ninety. Maybe the heat would break for the holiday tomorrow, which, as experience taught him, would be a good thing.

Tempers were short when people were hot, especially if alcohol was part of the mixture.

The Fourth of July celebration was a complete success.

The temperature at sunset was eighty-nine degrees and dropping quickly. Peck patrolled the fairgrounds and met up with Ed Kranston. The mayor was delighted.

"It's a record year for attendance," Kranston said. "I might even be able to balance the budget this year."

Peck lit a cigarette. "We could use a new squad car, Ed. Those 2015's we drive are showing their age."

"Contact Ford, see what kind of deal they have," Kranston said. "But, don't make any commitments. The council would have my ass."

Peck nodded. "Want to see the fireworks, Ed?"

"Why I'm here."

At the small racetrack in the center of the fairgrounds, thousands of people gathered, anticipating the start of the fireworks display. Peck and Kranston stood on the fringe of the crowd and watched the dark sky.

The blond-haired Deb Robertson was suddenly at Peck's side. "Hey, Dave."

"Hi, Deb. I thought you were at your booth," Peck said.

"I was. I closed it early. I love fireworks." Deb looked at Kranston. "Good evening, Mayor."

"How was business?" Kranston asked.

"Best year ever."

"Glad to hear it."

The fireworks began and the sky lit up in a dazzling display of colors and shapes. The show lasted forty-five minutes and drew loud cheers and applause from the massive crowd. During the finale, a barrage of rockets illuminated the sky so brightly, Peck could have read a newspaper.

As the sky darkened, ten thousand people cheered.

Kranston turned to Peck. "I'll be heading home, Dave. I'll see you in the morning."

"Goodnight, Mr. Mayor," Deb said.

Peck lit a cigarette and watched Kranston walk toward a fairground exit.

"Guess I'll be going home, too," Deb said. "Five a.m. comes awful early."

Peck nodded as he took a puff of his cigarette.

Deb looked at Peck. "You know, Dave. For ten months now, you stop by my diner every morning for coffee. We say our good mornings and you go on your way. What does a girl have to do to get you to ask her out?"

Peck hesitated, thrown by the question. "I don't know. I wasn't aware you wanted my attention."

Deb smiled as she shook her head. "Silly man. Walk me to my car and we'll talk about it."

At eleven, Peck and his men closed the fairgrounds. By the time money was cashed out and the grounds were secured it was after one. Peck dragged himself to his car and drove home, arriving at one-thirty. He was in bed and asleep by one forty-five.

Linda Boyce soaked in a hot tub full of scented water and oils. She puffed on a cigarette and sipped from a glass of wine while she waited for Ed to arrive. He said he would be there sometime after one a.m. She hated all the sneaking around, but Ed was a married man. Besides his wife to contend with, there was his reputation as mayor to worry about.

Therefore, she took the leftover crumbs and made do.

Linda stood up in the tub and reached for a white terrycloth towel on the rack. She dried herself and smelled her skin. Ed liked her to smell nice. It put him in a good mood and made him generous. Since he paid the rent on her home, she needed him to be very, very generous.

There was a gentle tapping at the front door and she let Ed in just after one a.m. He was in the mood and in a hurry, so they went to the bedroom and got right to it. He didn't even bother removing the damn gum from his mouth. That was okay with her. The quicker he got it out of his system, the quicker she could get some sleep.

He zeroed in on her at the fairgrounds and made the decision on the spot to follow her home. She had dark hair and eyes, a perfect ass and was exactly his type, which was female.

With the amount of people on the streets, it was easy to track her to her house on the fringe of town without attracting attention. Her house was set back off a dark side road where there were plenty of trees and shadows for concealment.

He waited. He was a patient man and was used to waiting. All good things come to those who wait, his mother would tell him when he was a boy. Little did mother know how right she was.

Lights went out and a lone candle flickered in the bedroom. The window was open to take advantage of the cooling, summer breeze. The damn hot spell had finally broken. Tonight was the first night he felt like venturing out.

Spotting her at the fairgrounds was a good omen. He felt it inside his head. He was going to get lucky.

As he waited, he checked the name on the mailbox mounted on a post by the end of the driveway. Linda Boyce. It was a nice name with a nice ring to it and he liked it.

He peeked in the bedroom window. She was taking a bath. He looked around and spotted a woodpile wedged between two trees. He selected a nice, two-foot-long log that had some weight behind it.

As he made his way around to the front door of the home, a car suddenly pulled into the driveway. A large man of about sixty exited the car and walked toward the front door. He caught a glimpse of the man's face in the floodlight over the front door. He recognized the man from around town. It was the mayor, Ed Kranston.

Fueled by a sudden, all-consuming rage, he pulled the ski mask from a back pocket and slipped it over his head.

Ed insisted on running the air conditioner even though it had cooled considerably. He hated to sweat during lovemaking, he insisted. She closed all the windows and ran the big one in the living room and the smaller one in the bedroom. What the hell, he was paying for it.

They slipped under the sheets. Even with the pill he took, Ed was slow to arousal, but after a while, he got there. He insisted on being on top and what the hell, he was paying for that, too. As Ed neared the edge, Linda closed her eyes. It was bad enough she would have to listen to him squeal, she did not need to see his eyes bulge like a frog.

The hum of the air conditioners masked all other noise. Linda heard the sound a moment too late and when she opened her eyes, a man in a ski mask was standing over them, holding a fire log.

Everything happened so fast, there was no time to react. The man in the ski mask struck Ed on the back of the head with so much force, Ed's skull split in two. Blood, skull and bits of brain matter hit her in the face and stuck to her skin.

Linda screamed and her first reaction was to jump, but Ed's bulk and dead weight pinned her down and she was helpless.

Linda saw the heavy log swinging in a high arc and that was the last thing on earth she would ever see.

★ ★ ★ ★ ★

Peck was asleep maybe a half hour when his cell phone, the private number used just for emergencies, rang on the bedside nightstand.

Instantly awake, Peck reached for the phone.

Reese spoke to him on the other end. "Dave, wake up. We got a bad one. A double murder."

Peck, Reese and several of his uniformed officers entered the residence of Linda Boyce and were shocked at the sight of the very grizzly, double homicide.

Ed Kranston, Mayor of Dunston Falls lay in a pool of his own blood on the bed. His skull was split open at the top and exposed bits of brain matter were everywhere.

A woman lay on her stomach next to Kranston. Her face had been beaten to a bloody pulp. Her features were unrecognizable. Her blood, like Kranston's, was everywhere, even the ceiling.

"Jesus Christ," Reese said.

Two of Peck's men went outside to vomit.

Peck said, "Do we know who the woman is?"

"A Linda Boyce, according to our computer and the mail on the kitchen table," Reese said. "That's all we know for now. I'm running a records check on her in the car."

Peck slipped on a pair of latex gloves. "Is Doctor McCoy on the way?"

"I called him right after I called you," Reese said.

Peck walked around the far side of the bed and picked up the heavy fire log. Dried blood and bits of skull clung to the wood.

"She has a woodpile out back?" Peck said.

"I don't know. Why?" Reese said.

"I'd like to know if he planned this out and brought this with him," Peck said and gently shook the log. "Or if something set him off and he decided to kill them on the spot."

Reese turned to one of the men. "Check it out."

The man nodded and left the bedroom.

"Who called it in?" Peck said.

"A neighbor," Reese said. "She said she heard a scream."

"I'll bet she did," Peck said. "Get someone over to the neighbor and take a statement. And where the hell is McCoy?"

"Should I call him again?" Reese asked.

"No. Get on the phone to the state police. Tell them we need a forensics team right away."

"You want to bring the state boys in on this?" Reese said. "You know they'll take over."

Peck turned to look at Reese. "We're pretty modern for a small town, but do you see a forensics lab anywhere around here?"

"No."

"Don't worry," Peck said. "We won't be left out in the cold, if that's what you're thinking."

"I'm thinking a murdered town mayor is news. Even in a small town like ours."

"Ed Kranston and a woman are dead. Think about that."

The officer sent to investigate the woodpile returned. "She has one out back. Logs just like that one. And Doctor McCoy is here."

McCoy, carrying a medical bag, entered the bedroom. He took one look around and said, "My good God, what the hell happened in here?"

"Somebody," Peck said, "was really, really pissed off about something."

In front of the Boyce home, Peck lit a cigarette and looked at Reese. "I'm going to the office to wait for the state boys. Nobody except Doctor McCoy goes in or out, right?"

Reese nodded and Peck walked to his cruiser and drove away. Reese stood on the front steps with the floodlight shining on him. Suddenly, the floodlight turned off and McCoy quietly exited the house. They stood in darkness and looked at each other. Reese sighed loudly to himself. McCoy cocked his head to look at Reese and in an instant, McCoy went from zero to sixty.

"Goddammit all," McCoy said in a sudden burst of fury. "Goddamn it all to hell."

Reese looked at McCoy and said nothing, knowing when to keep his mouth shut.

"Did you know about Ed and this woman?"

Reese shook his head. "After what happened the last time she was pulled from the program. She shouldn't even be here."

"Ed must have reinstated her for some reason on his own."

"I think I know what that reason is," Reese said.

"Christ, what the hell do we tell Washington?"

"We?" Reese said. "You're the boss, Tom."

"Ah, fuck me," McCoy said. "I spent five years reinventing that broken down drunken Kranston. Programming him to believe he is a respectable, government scientist in charge of a billion-dollar project. What the hell am I going to tell them, that my prize subject just had his brains mashed in while he was fucking a class B subject?"

Reese mulled it over in his mind before answering. "Tell them it's the perfect opportunity for Peck to act like a cop and catch the bad guy. He's the focal point of the whole thing after Kranston, anyway."

McCoy looked at Reese and slowly smiled. "Yeah. That's very good. That's exactly what I'm going to tell those assholes."

McCoy pulled a cell phone from a pocket, walked off the steps, and stood in the driveway to place a call.

Reese watched McCoy talk on the phone from the steps. He

reached into a pocket and withdrew a package of cigarettes wrapped in plain, white paper. He pulled one and lit it with a wood match.

McCoy finished his call and returned to the steps. He looked at the cigarette in Reese's hand. "Where did you get that? You know those are illegal."

"They're bootleg. I know this guy on the Canadian border," Reese said. "Besides, Peck smokes them all the time."

"That's how he gets his medication," McCoy said. "In small doses every time he lights up. Just like Kranston and his damned gum. You know that."

Reese let the cigarette fall to the steps where he crushed it under his shoe.

"Pick it up," McCoy said.

Reese picked up the butt and slipped it into a pocket. "So what did Washington say?"

"They said let him play cop," McCoy said. "They said to make it as stressful as possible. If Peck performs well, the project goes green light."

"This is so fucked up," Reese said. "We're supposed to let him run around with the state police and play detective?"

"That's exactly what we're supposed to do," McCoy said. "Get hold of what's her name playing Deb and tell her I want Peck seduced. Some sexual tension should add a bit more stress to the mix. Tell her to lay it on good. Then find out who is in the think tank nobody will miss. See if a few more victims to worry about will bring out the best in Mr. Peck."

"Or fuck him up," Reese said.

"Either way, we have to know. If a few murders and a blond cause deterioration, it will never work on some crazy dictator looking to rule the world."

"How do we know he'll kill again?" Reese asked. "This could be a one-time, isolated incident for him."

"I'm a doctor," McCoy said. "He trusts me. And even if he doesn't, he'll kill again because I want him to."

"Whatever happened to the good old days where we just shot the bad guys?" Reese said.

"Let's get some coffee," McCoy said. "You can tell me about those good old days when you were a young man in Iraq."

McCoy and Reese stepped off the front steps and walked toward McCoy's car.

"Hey," Reese said. "Who do we have available to play the state police?"

Peck entered the Dunston Falls Roman Catholic Church shortly before eight a.m. where he found Father Regan preparing the altar for the ten a.m. Sunday mass.

The priest was dressed in black pants with a matching shirt. Peck stood at the altar railing. "Father, I need to see you for a minute."

Regan nodded and set aside the candleholders he was polishing. He left the altar and met Peck in the front pew.

"I have the feeling this is about Ed Kranston and the woman," Regan said.

"You've heard?" Peck said.

"Doctor McCoy asked me to administer last rites. It came as quite a shock to me, a situation like that in our small town."

"In today's world, Father, no town, no matter how small or remote is safe from predators," Peck said. "It's just the way things are."

"Sadly, I have to agree with you. I suppose that is why people turn to the church more now than ever." Regan paused to look at Peck. There was sadness in his eyes. "Ed Kranston was a good man, a friend of mine and Linda Boyce was an active member of the church. Both of them will be missed."

Peck looked at Regan and nodded. "You'll be mentioning it

at the service?"

"Yes, but I will be delicate," Regan reassured Peck. "Even good, God-fearing people have their faults. Only God should judge them at the end."

Peck looked at the altar for several seconds. It was large and adorned with gold, trimmed with expensive, decorative lace. "Thank you, Father," Peck said.

Regan grinned at Peck. "For I have sinned," the priest joked.

Peck turned to the priest and smiled, the small joke not being lost on his cop's sense of humor. "Don't we all," Peck said.

Regan nodded and his tiny smile faded. "I will pray for you, Sheriff. For the strength and wisdom to catch this man before he can take another innocent life."

Peck stood up and gently placed a hand on Regan's shoulder. "Make it a good one, Father."

Peck stood on the front steps of the Linda Boyce residence while he waited for the state police to arrive. He was dog-tired and sipped coffee from a deli container, his fifth cup of the day. From inside the house, his second-in-command, Lieutenant Reese, limped out to join him.

"Everything is ready for the state boys," Reese said. "They should be here any minute."

Peck nodded and lit a cigarette.

Reese said, "Hey, can you spare one of those, Dave?"

Peck handed Reese his pack as a state patrol car arrived and entered the driveway. The man who exited the car looked vaguely familiar to Peck. He wondered where, if ever, their paths had crossed.

"I'm Detective Muse of Homicide," he said as he approached Peck.

Peck stared at the man as he puffed on his cigarette.

"I'm Sheriff David Peck," Peck said, extending his right hand to Muse.

"Show me what you got," Muse said.

Epilogue

Alone in his church, Father Regan sat for several long minutes and enjoyed the quiet solitude the sanctuary afforded him.

Suddenly, he sighed loudly to himself. Another headache was brewing, starting with a spot between his eyes. Probably from all the smoking he had been doing lately. Why did he ever start such a filthy habit? Gently, he massaged the spot with his left hand.

The pain began to subside and he stood up to return to the altar to continue polishing candleholders. He noticed a splinter in his right thumb that must have come from that damn log. He picked at it, but the splinter was in too deep.

The things people make me do, Regan told himself as he left the altar to dig out the splinter and prepare to say the ten a.m. mass.

ABOUT THE AUTHOR

Al Lamanda is a native of The Bronx. He has studied Security Management at NYU and Fire Safety at John Jay College and has specialized in Interviewing Techniques. He has worked for several major corporations in the Loss Prevention field, as well as Private Investigations. He presently lives in Maine where he has written three screenplays in addition to *Dunston Falls.* He is currently working on a new novel.